DARK HORSES

DARK HORSES

A Tale of the Arkadian Terror

SUZANNE THACKSTON

Cover and interior paintings by Claudia Tisdale
Author photograph by William Fox Photography

Copyright © 2019 by Suzanne Thackston

This book is dedicated to

Demeter Who Sends Forth Gifts,

Dark-Maned Poseidon,

Persephone the Star-Seed

and Hermes of the Winged Words.

Acknowledgements

Special thanks to Laura Golder Kenney for the brilliant editing, the Frederick Writers' Salon for the critiques and coaching, and to Tisdale Flannery for all the encouragement and love.

Contents

Chapter 1

DARK HORSE

DUSK IS CREEPING INTO THE CREVICES OF THE Arkadian mountains, but Kiri has not found her pregnant goat. Mist-maidens coil around her as she reaches the bank of the River Ladon. Tiny spring frogs sing like mainads in the dusk. Her bare feet sink into silky mud, cold and smooth. She stops for a moment, wriggling her toes. She whispers a greeting to the limnades of the marsh whose foggy fingers are curling her hair into Medusa tendrils.

This liminal time of day is dangerous. Creatures without kindness toward tender things walk the gloaming. But Kiri knows her local nymphs. She moves without fear through the woods that cluster along the river, as much at home as a fox. She does not plan to return home without her favorite goat, and with any luck, a newborn kid. The beating she would receive from her father for losing one of the herd is less motivation than her fierce protective love for her Amalthea.

The alabaster blue-eyed doe was a gift from Kiri's favorite uncle, and Kiri traded days of hard work trampling the olives for their oil in order to breed her to the best buck in the region. Distracted by a pair of mating hawks late in the afternoon, Kiri had let the doe slip away, probably looking for a private spot in which to kid. But she is not about to lose the foundation of her future herd to a mountain lion or wolf.

Or any other being.

The western sky erupts in a final paroxysm of glory, as the frogs' music shrills to ecstatic heights. Kiri holds her breath in wonder. Even her worry cannot prevent her from stopping to experience the fiery descent of Helios behind the western hills, and thence to the fabled sea beyond Elis. Kiri has heard such tales of the sea, but never seen it with her own eyes. She stands riveted until the fierce flames begin to soften. A three-quarter waxing moon is already high above the treetops, gravid as the women who come to seek the skills of Kiri's midwife mother.

She moves through the deepening dusk, feet sure, eyes keen in the deceptive moonlight, ears attuned to any noises not belonging to the woods. She has herded her family's goats her entire life and knows the sorts of nooks and crannies favored by a kidding doe.

Down past a crook in the river, a few miles from the upland meadow where Kiri grazes her goats, a thick copse of oak and cypress trees marks the river's path as it winds its way to the wider grasslands that stretch to the western hills. The shadows blur in the thickening purple light, but between the trees Kiri sees a flash of white. Quick as a hare, she flits across the field and slips into the deeper shadow of the still-bare oaks and brooding cypress. She stands motionless, quieting her breathing, peering into the gloom. Nothing. Where did it go?

The frogs fall silent.

Kiri freezes. She holds her breath. Her heart slams against her ribs.

Movement under the cypresses, just feet away. Whiteness looms, big, far too big to be Amalthea. Kiri staggers back a step, trying to breathe as the thing steps toward her. A branch cracks, shockingly loud in the silence.

She is staring into the dark eyes of a dapple-gray mare.

Kiri's breath whooshes out of her. The mare eyes her steadily, then shakes her head, her long forelock falling over her eyes. She thrusts out her nose and takes a suspicious sniff. Kiri stands still as a stone. She has seen the wild herds running on the river plains far below her pastures, but no one in her simple world can keep a tamed horse, and she has never been near the wild ones. Their fierce swift beauty has captivated her from afar, but they have been less a part of her world than the naiads and dryads who share her daily routines.

She had no idea how large they could be.

The delicate nostrils quiver inches from Kiri's face. Sweet, grass-scented breath blows over her, and she gasps. The mare jerks back and steps away, back under the trees, where her white and gray mottled hide nearly disappears against the dark and moonlit branches. Kiri remains motionless.

A single frog tentatively tries out its voice. Another joins it. In seconds the chorus is in full song. If Kiri did not know where to look she would think that she was alone in the night with the tiny creatures.

Almost without volition, she sinks to her knees. The terror is still there but has receded to the back of her brain, almost swamped by an awe as inexplicable as the fear.

Kiri kneels in the grass for what seems an eternity, deafened by the frog symphony, the gray horse motionless under the trees. She is content to remain thus until rosy-fingered Dawn brightens the east, but without warning the frogs fall silent again. The darkness under the trees seems to thicken. Kiri's heart begins to thud loudly in her ears again. Something small and warm scurries between her feet and they both freeze, prey animal instinct.

The mare's ears flatten.

Kiri can feel the earth vibrate beneath arrogant footfalls before she sees the massive silhouette loom against the sky. The tiny creature between her feet quivers. A snort ruptures the tense silence like a blast from a salpinx. Dread squeezes the last breath from Kiri's lungs. She prays her slamming heartbeats are not audible.

A massive hoof is raised high, paws the ground. The stallion neighs, deep, brassy, shattering the night air into shards of pure hysteria.

The silence thickens around Kiri like icy mud, trapping her in place. She wants to hide her head in her arms but she cannot move. She strains to see the motionless mare. But even the shadows are frozen.

The ground shudders again, hoofbeats like hammer blows coming nearer, coming faster. Kiri forces her eyes up, sees a mane like shredded silk rippling against the stars, a green gleam of eyes. The stallion pounds through the grass, coming directly for the copse, an inexorable tidal wave racing toward the shore.

A grunt of despair escapes the mare just before she bursts from the sheltering trees, arrowing out of the little grove, up onto the grassland, fleet as a shooting star. A high-pitched whinny floats back, shaking with fear and fury. Her slender legs reach impossibly far as she flees, her tail a bone-white blur in the moonlight. Kiri has never seen anything so fast, faster than a stooping hawk, far faster than the fleetest stag. Nothing could ever catch this wild being. She rivals the killing winds of Boreas.

But the thing pursuing her is more than hawk, or stag, or wind. The pounding hooves boom like an ocean storm-surge against a cliff. Cracks open in the shuddering earth beneath the onslaught of those hooves.

Breath rushes painfully back into Kiri's lungs. She swarms up the nearest oak, which until a moment before sheltered the dapple-gray mare. Gasping, trembling, she clutches at the trunk, staring out over the moonlit plain, riveted by the terrible pageant unfolding below.

The mare is quick as a cloud, skimming the grasses. The black bulk pursuing her seems too huge, too gross to be able to capture anything so quicksilver in the moonlight. But the space between them closes. The powerful legs of the stallion pummel the earth like pistons, causing Gaia Herself to groan. Kiri's eyes bulge with horror as she sees a wild boar, fleeing from the furious hooves, go tumbling into a newly-formed crack zig-zagging across the plain. It disappears with a surprised shriek.

The race is over. With a last mighty effort, the stallion is upon the mare. Huge jaws gape open, seize her by the crest of her straining neck and clamp down. He sits down on his massive haunches. The mare turns a somersault in the air, landing heavily, her breath driven from her laboring lungs. The immense form looms over her, motionless except for his heaving flanks. She gathers herself and lurches to her feet.

She faces him, ears flat, trembling. A despairing whinny of defiance bursts from her. The stallion stretches his head, touches her muzzle with surprising delicacy, then twines his neck around hers. They stand thus for a long moment. Then he moves behind her, rears and covers her, knees gripping her flanks, huge head laid along her neck. Their silhouettes undulate against the starry sky.

The stallion dismounts. The mare's knees buckle. She staggers, recovers, and turns to face him, flanks pumping like bellows. He shakes the forelock from his eyes and extends his muzzle toward her. Kiri can see the curve of his nostrils, limned in a phosphorescent green. For a long moment they stand motionless, the mare's head low, the stallion's nose almost touching her forehead. Then she flings her beautiful head high, ears flattened, and screams. She wheels and kicks violently, deadly hooves just missing the stallion's startled face. He leaps sideways, snorts explosively, trots in a tight circle, legs flung high. He halts and lowers his head toward the mare again, but now his ears are back too, and his eyes flash green. With a neigh that splits the night like a bronze trumpet, he spins and gallops off, hooves thundering. As he disappears over the horizon the cracks in the plain groan, and close.

The mare watches until he is out of sight, eyes blazing in the moonlight, ears still pinned flat against her neck. When he is gone, and the ground has stopped shaking from the mighty passage, she lets out a deep sigh. Her head droops to the ground.

Kiri makes her way down the tree, slowly, wanting to go to the mare, but afraid to the marrow of her bones. As she steps hesitantly from the copse onto the grass of the plain, the moon slips behind a cloud. The world goes dark. Kiri peers through the gloom, trying to make out the dappled hide, but the stars do not illuminate the night enough for her to see. She hesitates, wringing her hands unconsciously as she has seen her mother do in times of stress and uncertainty. Going forward into the darkness seems unthinkable. But Kiri cannot bring herself to leave the mare, ravaged and alone, in the sea of grass.

She stumbles forward in the dark, mouth dry, breath coming in ragged gasps. The long grass tangles her feet, impeding her passage. She halts, trying to quiet her breath, to get her bearings in the grass, perhaps to find the mare by sound if not by sight. But the only sound in the night is the wind rustling the waving stalks of last year's dried grain.

After what seems an eternity of nightmare, Kiri catches sight of the mare not far ahead. An ear twitches at the sound of Kiri's approach. The mare swings her head around menacingly. Kiri freezes. She tries desperately to think of some way of assuring the mare of her good intentions, but she can only think to fall to her knees, hands outstretched imploringly. Time freezes. The two creatures seem carved of stone in their tableau.

Eventually the moon slips out from its curtain of cloud. Kiri gasps. The sea of grass around them silvers in the moonlight, but the mare remains dark. No light reflects back from the mane that was silvery-white. The deep dapples have dimmed and bled together. The mare's body has become a complete darkness, like gazing into a well. The eyes, so limpid in the grove, now glare into Kiri's, rimmed in red. As they stare at each other, black flames eat their way into Kiri's mind, and she swoons into the receiving grass.

When Kiri opens her eyes the stars have fled. Eos touches the eastern horizon with pearl, although the plain is still swathed in darkness. She is alone in the grass.

Wearily she pulls herself to her feet and begins the long trudge back. The mare is gone. Amalthea is gone.

Her goats are scattered. Her parents will be frantic, and she will certainly be beaten when she gets home. But all that she can think of is the terrible change in the mare, from pearl gray beauty to dark horror.

The chariot of the sun has not risen above the horizon, but the world is full of dawnlight as Kiri reaches the grove where just the night before, a lifetime ago, a beautiful horse sheltered under the trees. The birds are beginning to wake and sing. Woven through the dawn chorus is the croaking of ravens. Kiri raises her tired eyes and sees a trio perched on the top branches of an oak, focused on something near the river. She follows their gaze, spies something white, and a fitful movement.

The body of Amalthea lies partially in the water, the gentle current tugging at her limp legs, giving her a ghastly appearance of life. Kiri halts, unable to believe what her eyes are telling her. She remains still for so long that one of the ravens, emboldened, swoops down and lands heavily on the still-warm body. Kiri screams, runs forward waving her arms madly, and the startled raven leaps up with a cry of frustration. Kiri falls beside the still body of the white goat and gathers the delicate head onto her lap, rocking, keening. The blood and viscera by Amalthea's hindquarters make all too clear the cause of death. Flies are already gathering.

Kiri gazes down into the beloved face, the blue eyes

half-lidded and milky in death. She is sure her heart will break. She ululates more loudly, sending the ravens spiraling into the sky, but the flies buzz and cluster ever more greedily.

The sun is flooding the plain with golden light as Kiri's howls falter and die in exhaustion. She pushes away from the stiffening body and stands, looking around for sturdy branches to make a toboggan. Her precious doe can feed her family for a week if she can get her home before decay sets in, and it is her responsibility to make sure that the little goat does not go to waste. She sees a good strong bough sticking out of a clump of reeds near the water and trudges wearily to grasp it and begin making her sled. But as she begins to tug she hears a faint, wavering bleat. She spins round and stares at the reeds, seeing them ripple ever so slightly. Her breath catches in her throat. She plunges into the reeds, and there, on the bank, curled around each other, are two tiny, perfect kids, one pure white, the other midnight black. At her intrusion, they begin to cry weakly, pitifully, butting each other with tiny, desperate muzzles.

Once again Kiri finds herself on her knees, but this time weeping with painful joy. She gathers the warm little creatures onto her lap where they snuggle like kittens, trying frantically to nurse. Kiri has nothing to feed them save the watered wine in her wineskin. She dips a fold of her khiton into the skin and gives it to the babies to suck, but it quietens them only for a moment. She knows she has to get them home.

In a matter of moments, she has assembled a makeshift sledge of tree limbs bound with reeds. Amalthea's pitiful body is secured and wrapped in more reeds to keep out the flies. Kiri cannot bring herself to set the babies next to their mother's bloating body. She slings the white kid over her shoulders, tucks the black one under one arm, grasps the branches of her toboggan, and begins the weary hike back up to the highlands, to her home. She hopes her goats have made their way home, that her herd dogs have kept them together and alive. But she cannot dwell on that, nor on what awaits her in the hut where her parents will be hard-handed in their anger and relief at seeing her. It takes every bit of strength she possesses to make her way along the river path to the upland meadows with her burdens. Her heart is sore at the loss of Amalthea, and she is full of fear lest she lose the babies as well, the precious, precious babies.

And underneath it all, the grief and the exhaustion and the worry and the relief, runs the memory of that night flight, the green flash of the stallion's eyes, and the red darkness of the mare.

Chapter 2

BRINGING FORTH

RAIN DRUMS ON THE HOOD OF KEPHALOS'S CLOAK, made of good fox fur that yet soaks miserably through. The lower plains of Arkadia are merely chilly and damp, but high in this northern mountain region the rain has ominous knife-edges of ice, and the wind is cruel. Nothing but his frantic fear for his wife would bring him out on such a night. She has come early to her childbed, and this is their first, and she is so small.

The home of Stephanos and Aglaia lies far below Kephalos's mountain cave, but Aglaia is famed throughout their sparsely populated region for bringing women and babes through the birthing ordeal alive.

The early evening darkness is thick. No torch could survive this bitter night. Kephalos knows his mountain paths, but the rain and wind and darkness conspire to make his journey slick and perilous. His knees are bruised already from two hard falls, and he battles to keep his panic at bay, to slow his speed. A broken ankle will not help his little wife.

As he navigates the faint rocky trail he prays fervently to both Artemis Orsilokhia and Eleuthyia to watch over his wife and baby, and curses the bad luck that has caused Eleni to begin her labor at such an inauspicious time. They have been saving olive oil and wine for Aglaia's midwifery gifts, and still reckoned on another full moon phase before it would be time to invite her into their home to await the ordeal. He left his white-faced whimpering wife alone over an hour ago, and it will be another hour before he reaches his destination. Then Aglaia will need to pack her medicinals and charms, and make the steep climb back up in the dark, which will take far longer than his precipitous flight down to the upland plain. First babies often arrive slowly. But can Eleni hold on until they return?

The wind whips into his eyes, stinging and blurring. At first, he thinks the tiny, distant light may be nothing more than tears and hope, but he wipes his eyes with a sleeve beaded with icy droplets, and it continues to beckon him down the mountain. Aglaia's cottage is finally in view. He cannot tell if it is tears or sleet that streak his face.

Before he can reach the door, he is stopped by the

warning growl of the herd dogs, and he can see them lined up in the dim, damp yard, four of them, hackles spiked, lips rippling back from gleaming teeth.

"Ho! Aglaia! Stephanos! Call off your beasts, it is I, Kephalos!" A moment later, firelight floods the slippery patch of earth before the threshold. He is drawn into the warmth of the tiny home and its flickering hearthfire. Outside, the dogs whine in disappointment and return to their watch outside the goats' pen.

"Gods above and below, Kephalos, Hermes himself must be perched on your head to have guided you down in this weather! What could bring you out on such a cursed night? Here, Kiri! Warm some wine for our guest! Karissa, bring water for him to wash! Is there bread?" Stephanos helps him out of his sopping cloak and hangs it near the fire, wafting steam into the room.

Gratefully, Kephalos sinks onto a stool before the fire, stretching his hands and feet to its warmth. Little Karissa hurries over with a wooden basin of water and kneels at his feet while he washes. She gently begins to draw his goatskin boots from his feet, but he halts her, scattering water droplets, suddenly terrified that these scant moments spent taking his comfort will doom his errand.

"No time, no time for wine or rest, Stephanos! Where is Aglaia? Eleni's time is at hand, and I need to bring your wife back up the mountain or she will die! She is so small, Stephanos, and the babe comes too soon. Aglaia!"

Kiri turns from the kettle over the fire, her face frozen in shock. The ladle with which is she warming the wine clatters to the hearthstones. Karissa, mouth hanging wide, retrieves the ladle and whisks it and the lustration bowl out of the way. She retreats to a dark corner of the tiny room, drawing a small boy of no more than two against her side.

Stephanos's bushy brows snap together, his deep voice rumbling with dismay as he replies.

"Kephalos, my friend, Aglaia was called away yester eve to the gathering down by the river for the Lenaia festival. A woman is brought to childbed there, and no midwives near. We did not expect to hear from you for yet another moon."

"I know! I, too! But the child comes, timely or not, and Eleni cannot manage the birthing without help. Oh, Stephanos, what am I to do? There is no one else, and the Lenaia gathering is too far. We could never make it back to her in time!"

Kiri's eyes meet her father's across the bowed back of the despairing man. He gazes at her steadily, then nods. Briskly, she returns to the kettle of warm spiced wine, ladles some into a bowl and thrusts it into Kephalos's hands.

"Here, drink this. You need to restore your

strength. I have helped my mother before, I will come with you and help Eleni bring her child into the world."

Kephalos takes the wine numbly, staring at her.

"You? But, Kiri, you are just a child yourself. How can you—"

He breaks off, seeing her as if for the first time. She is no longer a little maiden, but fully thirteen years old, ready for marriage and children of her own. The skinny wild-haired girl whom he has seen scampering over the mountains with her goats now looks back at him with serious eyes, and a calm demeanor.

"I have not assisted at a birth without my mother there to supervise, it is true," she says, "but I have been present and helped her many, many times. And there is no one else. Wait but a moment while I gather what we will need, and I will come with you."

While Kiri begins loading strips of coarsely woven cloth, pads of wool and bags of herbs into a basket, Kephalos bemusedly accepts a clean rag and dries himself roughly before the fire. He swallows the bowl of wine in two great gulps and begins pulling on his still-damp and steaming outerwear. By the time he is ready, Kiri is beside him, a sharp bone knife wrapped and tucked into the bottom of her neatly packed basket. Stephanos himself fetches her warm cloak and wraps it snugly around her. She smiles at this gesture of solicitousness from her normally imperturbable father, and leans against him for a moment, savoring his warmth and strength. He tilts her face up to him and gazes searchingly into her eyes.

"Little thistle, you have grown much in the last year. Ever since you came back without your white goat and with the two kids, you have been different. And not just because you are becoming a woman." He sighs. "This is a woman's task, and I would not have it fall to you, but you bring pride and honor to our home by taking it on." He presses his forehead briefly to hers. "You are my good girl. Go, and do what you can for Eleni. May the gods go with you."

She flings her arms around his neck, then turns to the wide-eyed children pressed against each other in the corner.

"Karissa, Patrokles, be good, and help Father. Tend the fire, and make sure the goats are cared for. Mother will return soon." She kisses them swiftly, then turns to Kephalos, who is waiting impatiently by the door. "Sir, have you a torch?"

He replies roughly, "No torch will stay lit on such a night, girl! I know my way. Follow me closely, and make haste!" And with a whirl of wind and wet, the door opens, then closes behind them.

The long, dreary night is barely half-spent when the two soaked, freezing, exhausted travelers reach the dimly-lit entrance to a small cave, high in the Parnon mountains. It is mercifully sheltered from the worst of the winds by a massive outcropping that blocks the northern elements. The fitful flicker of a dying fire draws the tired pair up the final approach, but they look at each other worriedly at the silence. No moans of a woman in labor, nor yet the wails of a newborn reach their ears above the hiss of the sleet.

"Eleni," breathes Kephalos as he steps into the narrow opening, drawing Kiri beside him, eyes frantically searching the dim interior. Only a few coals glow in the crude hearth. A heap of furs lies in a careless pile before the fire. It is brutally cold and damp, the walls dripping with condensation, but after the terrible climb in the storm it feels like a haven. But Kiri has no time to appreciate the relative stillness, the slight suggestion of warmth. She sees a limp, white hand extended from under the furs, deathly still. With a muffled exclamation she pushes forward, and gently pulls the furs back from the small woman who lies there, eyes closed, belly grossly swollen.

"Build up the fire, quickly, you fool!" she hisses at Kephalos, all respect due to an adult man forgotten by both as she falls to her knees and begins examining the still form. Glancing desperately over his shoulder as he works, Kephalos obeys her unquestioningly, bringing armfuls of dry wood from the back of the cave and blowing gently on the embers to cause them to flare and dance. He notes with dread that almost none of the pile of logs and twigs left next to the hearth for Eleni to use in his absence have been burned. It is a miracle that the fire did not altogether die.

When the flames are leaping and crackling again, and some degree of light and warmth begins to steal into the dark cave, Kephalos dares ask the question burning behind his lips.

"Kiri, is she dead? Is my Eleni dead?" He cannot yet think about the babe.

Kiri's answering smile is swift as she glances at him, before she turns her attention back to the still form, a worried frown returning to her brow.

"No, but Hekate Psykhopompos is near. Eleni is senseless, but her body yet works to expel the child. Can you heat some water for me? I must clean her so that I can examine her, and help the child from the birthing canal. Pray! Pray to Artemis to keep her back from the brink!"

The two of them gently reposition Eleni near the fire on clean furs, Kephalos bundling the soiled, partially frozen ones and tossing them unceremoniously out of the cave. He crouches by his wife's head, holding her small, boneless hand in his large one, stroking her hair, murmuring unintelligibly to her. Kiri kneels between the sprawled legs, washes her hands in a small basin of warmed water and herbs, then coats her right hand in olive oil from a vial in her basket. With her left on the woman's abdomen, feeling for the ripple of contractions, she gently works her right hand into the birth canal, making her way toward the baby. She flashes a quick smile at Kephalos.

"I feel the head. The baby is positioned correctly, and the cord is not wrapped around the neck. If we can ease it out, we may save Eleni yet."

"And the child?"

"I don't know. I can't know until it's born. Ah! Here comes a birth pang! Kephalos, let loose Eleni's hand and listen. Put your hands here—thus, on her belly—and when I say, push. She is too weak and has lost so much blood. We must help her expel this child."

They work together in the red light, the wind's howl distant and barely noticed. And some time later, in the deep dark of night, Kiri's oiled hands pull the limp, tiny baby from between Eleni's inert thighs.

Kiri finds that the routine she has learned from her mother takes over. She clears the baby's mouth and nose, pressing lightly on the chest, finally placing her own mouth over the small face and breathing gently into the open mouth. Her heart leaps when she sees the ribcage rise and fall, ever so slightly, and hears a gurgle no louder than a kitten's mew. A quick glance, and she catches Kephalos's eyes and smiles into them.

"Your daughter lives, at least for moment. Take her, sir, and massage her gently. Wrap her in this fur, here, keep her warm, and keep rubbing her. I must see to Eleni. Her labor is not yet done."

As Kiri works over the unconscious form of Eleni,

she can hear Kephalos's soft sobs and murmurs as he cradles his new daughter. And as Kiri slides the placenta out of Eleni's body, she is gratified to hear a tiny, plaintive wail. The wavering sound fills the small cave.

A weak voice whispers from the furs by the fire, "Kephalos? Is that our baby?" and is answered by a great noise, half roar, half sob.

Smiling, Kiri slides an arm under Eleni and lifts her to a slightly raised position, resting her shoulders on the bunched furs, then removes the baby from Kephalos's arms and places her on Eleni's drastically deflated belly.

"Here is your new daughter, brave Eleni. Your birth milk is in. Put her to your breast, and feed her. She has had a difficult journey."

As Eleni nurses her baby in wonder, Kiri finishes washing her, packs absorbent wool between her thighs, and winds strips of cloth around her hips to hold it in place. The bloody furs are moved aside, and the clean ones which Kephalos has ready are wrapped around mother and child, who barely notice the fuss and solicitude, so rapt are they with each other.

It is imperative that blood and effluvium of the birth be cleaned and removed from the area of the cave lest predators are attracted. Wearily, Kiri washes the placenta and places it in a kettle to be boiled for broth to nourish the new mother after her ordeal, and then begins the unpleasant task of gathering the unsalvageable furs and finding a suitable spot for disposal. Digging a hole is not an option in the icy wet night, and it is too treacherous to simply find a far place to abandon them. Fortunately, there is a steep cliff around the mountain's shoulder and not much higher than the cave's entrance. With a cry for the offering to be accepted by Eleuthyia and Artemis, Kiri flings the sodden, strong-smelling bundle into the winds, followed by a fervent prayer of thanks.

The wind is no less sharp, but the stinging pellets of sleet have subsided by the time Kiri has finished the birthing broth and presented it to the exhausted but elated Eleni. Kiri also makes sure there is food prepared for the new father, plenty of wood for the fire, and a clean stack of fresh wool pads and furs so that mother and child can stay clean and dry. As Kiri packs her basket, Kephalos looks up from his wife and daughter with stricken dismay.

"Kiri, you must stay! You cannot walk home alone in this darkness, but I cannot leave Eleni and the baby. We have gifts, too, the gifts we have put aside for Aglaia are yours; I must carry them down for you. Stay, and rest!"

But Kiri shakes her head.

"Mother may not return today, and there is work to do. Father is taking some of the goats for trade, and the little ones are not yet able to tend to the rest on their own. I can make my way home without help, and when Eleni is strong enough to be on her own, you can bring the doula gifts to us. The rain and sleet have stopped. I will be fine."

Nothing they say can dissuade her and Kephalos and Eleni are too wrapped up in their new child to protest for long. Soon, Kiri is on her way down the mountain, warmed by a draught of spiced wine, fortified by a strip of dried meat and a morsel of bread, her feet securely tied into a handsome new pair of goatskin boots.

An occasional star peers through the ragged wrack of clouds as Kiri works her way along a path so narrow and stony it is barely visible in full daylight. Sure-footed as she is, she moves her feet carefully forward, testing each step before putting weight on it, watchful for loose rocks and jagged thorns. No snakes will venture forth in the damp cold, but other dangers walk the mountains, and Kiri is alert despite her exhaustion.

But even though Kiri knows the local mountain pathways well, a dark stormy night with no sleep can fool the most experienced traveler. At a point where she expects to be halfway home, Kiri is dismayed to find that instead of the cedar grove she should be entering, she is being led by the tiny path deeper into the mountain fastness. The soaring buttresses of stark stone rising around her are entirely unfamiliar. She halts, puts a hand to her head, tries to get her bearings.

The footing is so treacherous that she has had to focus on each step she has taken, trusting her instincts to guide her down the right path. Has she made a mistake? At no point does the path she knows wind so, in such unfathomable patterns.

Kiri stands in the midst of strange escarpments, so tall that the black sky is almost blotted out. Even the wind has not followed her into this place. The silence is profound.

When the moaning begins, Kiri at first thinks it is the wind, or perhaps her tired brain recalling Eleni's faint moans as her senseless body did its work without her volition. And almost without volition Kiri lifts her head and follows the sound.

Boulders and broken rocks litter the ground, making an already difficult terrain even harder to navigate. Kiri inches her way forward, using her stout stick to feel ahead before she takes a step. Even with the good skin boots on her feet, they are battered and sore, and Kiri is cold and exhausted. Yet she keeps moving forward over the loose scree, stabbed by broken shrubs and thorn bushes, trying not to twist an ankle on a rolling rock. As she feels her way around an outcropping of stone, her hand encounters emptiness. She stands at the mouth of a cave.

A drawn-out groan shivers around her.

A faint gleam, like no light Kiri has ever seen before, illuminates the back of the cave, indicating a narrow passageway. She stares at the dim, green glow, a memory stirring deep in her subconscious and, with it, a twist of terror. Her heart seems to lurch to a halt, then start up again with slow, irregular slams. But she takes another step, then another, working her way to the back of the cave, to the cold, dim glow.

The passage leads back, and down, into the guts of the mountain. The rock walls are cold and slick. Kiri makes her way for some time—she does not know how much—the passageway lit by the eldritch light, which does not ease her fear. After a few minutes, or an eternity, Kiri steps into an open space. The walls fall away from her questing fingers. The ceiling gapes above her.

A horse is lying in the center of floor, grunting softly. Its neck is stretched out, nostrils flared, while the long tail swirls over the hard stone floor. The distended abdomen ripples, and Kiri can see the push of membrane against the straining vulva. The horse is a mare, and she is about to give birth.

Black eyes rimmed in red meet Kiri's. An explosive snort echoes throughout the rock chamber as the mare swings her head up in warning. But another contraction seizes her, and her head drops back to the hard floor with a sigh. Her hind legs jerk taut, then scrabble. The pale green light intensifies for a second, then dims. Kiri stares in shock. The dark mottled hide, the tangled, matted mane, the beautifully-shaped head explode in her brain with a memory she has tried so hard to forget. The memory of a dappled mare made of moonlight and pearl, the mare from the plain on the way to sea, the mare who went dark on a night of wonder and terror.

The mare strains, her groans emanating like distant rolls of thunder. Kiri is rocked from her fearful stasis by the sight and sound of a birthing mother in crisis. Before she can think, she finds herself kneeling at the mare's hindquarters, reaching without looking into her basket for her olive oil and soft wool pads. Gently she cleans the blood and effluvium from the vulva. As the next contraction wracks the mare, she can see a pair of small hooves protrude from within the membrane, then recede away again. Kiri takes a deep breath, searches in her basket for the carefully-wrapped knife, and silently awaits the next contraction. Normally she would stroke the animal, murmur reassurance, perhaps even sing softly, but she does not dare touch or speak to this creature. Her tongue seems glued to the roof of her mouth with fear, even as her hands go about their accustomed work.

When the tough membrane again protrudes, Kiri is ready. She makes a short, quick incision, causing the mare to jerk and grunt, and now can reach in and grasp the small, soft hooves and prevent the body of the little creature from receding back into the mare. At the next contraction she pulls hard, bringing the forelegs and a small twitching nose out into the air. Three more contractions, and a wet black foal slides onto the cavern floor.

The mare is up in a trice. Kiri scrambles back against the wall, pulling her basket with her, out of reach of the sharp hooves and wicked teeth. The dark mare tears at the membrane covering the limp little form, then begins licking it roughly, nostrils rippling, small grunts and nickers bursting from her as she works. In moments the foal sits up, wavers, slides down again. But it perseveres, and after a few tries, stands on ridiculously long, wobbly legs, mewling like a kitten. The mare turns broadside to the foal, bumps its little sea-horse head with her stifle. The baby reaches under her and begins to nurse.

For long moments the only sound in the green-lit chamber is the greedy sucking of the little black foal, and the soft whickers of the mare. Her fear momentarily forgotten, Kiri watches in wonder, which grows to amazement as she notices that the tiny, furiously switching tail is the same eerie green as the cavern light. And with that realization, fear falls back on her like a heavy cloak.

At her intake of breath the mare's head swings to regard her with obsidian eyes. There is no vestige of warmth or pity in their black, fire-rimmed depths. But before Kiri can scream, or faint, or beg for mercy, she is released from the lock of those eyes. The mare nudges the foal, now slow and sated, from her udder. It rubs its milk-slobbered muzzle on her flank, then slides slowly to the floor, and in less than a minute is asleep, tiny flanks rising and falling contentedly. With a groan, the mare too falls to her knees, then heavily onto her side. But not to rest.

The hard ripples of birth contractions again begin to seize the mare. Kiri frantically cleans her hands on a twist of wool and crawls back to her position at the mare's hindquarters.

Something is thrusting its way out of the opening, but there is no membrane, or shape of tiny hooves. What is emerging from the straining mare is a shapeless, sinuous mass of shadow. It writhes, wet, and spills onto the cave floor, flowing like vapor. The mare screams once, then falls silent. Kiri's outstretched hands touch the glutinous, gleaming darkness, and she too screams, weakly, miserably, at the shock of cold. She scoots back, duty forgotten, everything forgotten, desperate only to get away from the heaving shadow, clutching her stricken hands in her lap. The impossible mass slips out of the straining body of the mare and lies quivering on the floor of the cave. It seems both solid as freshly spilled viscera, and as wispy as mist. Kiri tries to focus on it, but her eyes skitter away from the nightmare thing.

The mare slowly, slowly heaves herself to her feet. The flames of her eyes flare, then burn dim. The foal sleeps peacefully at her feet, tiny ribcage rising and falling rhythmically. The mare turns to her second-born, and begins to lick the mass. Wet whispers fill the cave.

Kiri wonders if she is going mad. She sees, without understanding, the emerging form of a girl-child.

After a few minutes, or another eternity, the whispering ceases. The mare stands motionless. At her forefeet lies an impossible thing.

Kiri is staring at the tiny body of a newborn baby girl, as perfectly formed as the little one she left in the high mountain cave. Except that the fragile neck ends in the head of a foal.

Its eyes are closed. The baby ribcage barely lifts and falls.

The mare is perfectly still, except for the flaming eyes which blink slowly, fixed on her daughter. When the placenta slides out, unheeded, it hits the cave floor with a wet glopping sound that startles a small shriek from Kiri's throat. But the mare does not so much as twitch an ear her way. Her terrible gaze never wavers from her child.

The tiny nostrils flutter. The tightly-shut eyelids tremble. Kiri's fingers dig into rock.

"You should leave." The voice is male, pleasant, slightly musical.

Kiri's head snaps around, finds no one there, then her eyes widen as she sees the black colt, still lying on the floor of the cave near the mare, now awake, head up, looking at her. He tosses the greenish forelock out of his eyes. The lips pull back in a ghastly semblance of a grin.

"Listen to me, little doula. My sister will be fully present very shortly now. I'm afraid she won't show gratitude for your service."

Kiri chokes. The mare takes a step back. A hind hoof lands in her placenta with a squish. The nightmare on the ground emits a gasping sound.

"Go." The green in the colt's eyes intensifies. "Now."

Kiri scrambles backwards, only just remembering to grab her basket as she puts as much distance between herself and the nativity tableau as she can. Never daring to take her eyes away, she backs into the passage. But before she can completely escape, the colt heaves itself to its feet on legs that are already less spindly, more sturdy, holding up a body bigger and more mature.

"The path to this place is deceptive. I will send you a guide. Follow it faithfully, and be back on your familiar road before Helios drives his chariot over the horizon. Do not dawdle." A disturbing lilt of laughter underlies the smooth voice. "A clever girl like you might escape the labyrinth unaided, but we won't chance it." In a more serious tone it continues, "You have done well this night, little doula. Whatever happens, remember that."

The green light intensifies. Kiri turns and flees.

At the mouth of the cave she trips over something, almost falls hard, catches herself just in the nick of time. She turns to see something vaguely shaped like a large stone, but with the faint green glow that is now both familiar and terrifying. She stifles a scream before making out the shape of a mountain tortoise, blinking wise eyes at her under its faintly gleaming shell. She understands. As it turns and begins to make off at a surprisingly swift pace, she follows.

The path turns and twists, doubles back on itself, wraps around boulders and scree. Exhausted, mind numb with fear, Kiri is sure that the night is endless, and that she is trapped in some dark dream from which she can never escape. So when the tortoise stops and cranes its wrinkled head back at her, she numbly waits for the next horror to befall her. Her bleary eyes slowly take in a familiar landmark, an ancient knotted pine with a deep crevice in its roots, and she realizes there is a faint gray light emanating from beyond a mountain path that she knows. The tortoise, no longer looking like anything other than a typical mountain tortoise, lumbers slowly off.

Kiri takes a deep breath, and, trembling, looks behind her. The path she knows continues up the mountainside. Nothing looks different or unfamiliar at all. There is no sign of the tortuous road which has taken her from the cave of dread.

Kiri turns her face from the mountain, and walks home in the growing light.

Chapter 3

THE DAWNING
OF THE DARK

LYKEION STEPS OUT OF THE WOODS, ADJUSTING his loin wrap. He feels himself flushing as a group of girls wreathed in early flowers for the Mounykhia festival walk past, giggling. He settles his lyre more firmly on his shoulder and raises his chin, resolving not to look at the gaggle of maidens with their bold eyes and bolder whispers. He strides away, but cannot quite resist a peek back over his shoulder as he approaches the festival crowd, and is rewarded by peals of tinkling laughter.

His cheeks are still hot as he takes his place among the other musicians readying themselves for the procession. His friend Hyakinthos nudges him with a drumstick.

"What were you up to in the woods, old man? I hope she was worth it! You look like you've been caught with your hand in the honeycomb." He winks. "I know you haven't been to a festival on your own before, but you seem to be learning quickly. Your old mentor must have passed on more than music before he died."

"Taking a piss, if you must know," he snarls. "Why does everyone find it so amusing?"

"Ho ho! 'Everyone,' eh? Sorry to hit you on a bruise, my friend! And no one can bruise you like a tender maiden can."

Lykeion scowls, but his friend's smile is infectious, and in a moment he is grinning sheepishly. "I subdued the beast in my breeches before he could frighten the fawns. But it was a battle worthy of Apollon himself!"

Hyakinthos rolls his eyes, but his retort is lost as the kitharas, pipes, drums and lyres take up a wild, skirling tune, and the maidens dance into midst of the musicians.

Later, after the rites have been performed, the libations poured, the sacrifices made, and the maidens have danced themselves to a standstill, Lykeion takes the place of honor next to the fire in the deepening dusk. His fingers caress the lyre strings, and a riffle of light notes sail off into the darkening air. He tells the tale of Artemis petitioning her Father for divine favors, including the title Phosphoria, a bringer of light in darkness.

"And thus we worship Her in this guise tonight, as Selene swells to ripeness, and we sing Her hymns and praises in the silver moonlight." He finishes with a flourish.

The audience is rapt, spellbound by his voice. Lykeion looks up, pleased with himself as he ends his tale with a dreamy series of chords, reveling in the effect of his bardcraft. Hyakinthos claps him on the shoulder as he replaces him in the honor seat, and Lykeion wanders off to find a full wineskin.

Drinking deep of a barely-watered blood-red brew, he feels the fumes rise to his head and laughs out loud at the moonbright sky. His earlier embarrassment evaporates. He is young, it is spring, there is wine, and there are girls. People are smiling, nodding, calling out to him as he walks through the throng, staggering only slightly as he waves back, acknowledging the praise. Not since he was a small boy, before he left his mother's home to take up his apprenticeship, has he so enjoyed a festival. The Arkadian mountains during the Mounykhia are a fine place to be.

The lilt of girls' voices and the sound of bells catches his attention. A little off to the side, in a clearing of graceful silver-barked birch trees, a small circle of girls chants softly. Their bodies sway ever so slightly, their white robes glimmering like the trees, as if they were dryads themselves. Into their center walks a tall girl carrying a round cake. Around the rim are tiny twigs afire with bright flames, creating a circle of brightness. The girl walks slowly, carrying her offering with reverence, and white flowers are bound to her brow.

The girls part and form two lines, still chanting, tiny silver bells chiming on their fingers. The offering is carried between them to a simple stone shrine covered with branches and flowers. As the full moon's light moves through the trees and pours over the shrine, the tall girl sets down the ritual cake called the amphiphontes, the shining-all-around cake. The voices raise to a high, pure note of ecstasy as the celebrants raise their arms to the sky. Suddenly the ritual is over, and the girls resume their everyday aspects, running back to the crowds giggling and shouting, arms entwined around each others' waists. Only the tall girl remains, standing before the shrine, head bent, long hair cascading before her face.

Something about her manner catches Lykeion's attention. She seems a little older than the other girls, but that is not what arrests him. Her lowered head, the slight slump of her narrow shoulders strike a note of sorrow in his bard's heart. He is suddenly consumed by a fierce need to find out what is causing her pain.

Before he can follow his thoughts his feet are carrying him forward into the clearing, not knowing what he wants to say to her, but unable to stop himself. At the sound of his footfalls behind her she pushes her hair back with both hands and turns to face him.

Lykeion smiles his most charming smile, shoving down a frisson of unaccustomed shyness. He angles his body slightly so that his lyre is very visible, making his honored profession clear without being so crass as to point it out. He holds his breath as he watches her wide eyes touch his, then move to the lyre. Maybe she will speak to him, and the awkwardness of the first words will be behind them, and he can bedazzle her with his wit and words and music, and the strange breathlessness which has seized him will dissipate, and she will be just a pretty girl who has fallen under his spell. She will smile, laugh, sing to his music, flirt with him, and the moonlit night will pass pleasantly.

This scenario plays out so delightfully in Lykeion's head that he is nonplussed when the girl's eyes slide past him indifferently. She turns back to the shrine, whispers a final prayer, and blows out the few tiny twigs not already extinguished by the fresh evening breeze. Without a word she walks past him, not into the crowds, but into the trees. Her pale robe glimmers like a moonbeam between the white trunks of the birches, and then she is gone.

Lykeion finds himself back among the dwindling crowd, a disconsolate wanderer. The girl has taken all the festival bonhomie with her, leaving him feeling flat.

Seeing Hyakinthos passing around a wineskin with some of the other musicians, he decides to join them and forget her in the rough comfort of male companionship.

But as he approaches the little group he is surprised by the hushed tones of their voices, the absence of laughter, the somberness of the faces. He slips quietly among them, trying to pick up on the timber of the conversation without interrupting it. A man he has never seen before is speaking quickly, almost in a whisper. Lykeion takes a seat silently next to Hyakinthos and leans forward, listening intently.

"I've not encountered any tales from the east, on the plains, but the folk of the highlands and mountains are full of them. Children gone missing, screams in the night, eyes in the forest. Shepherds are starting to watch in pairs and groups; no one wants to be out at night with the flocks alone."

An older man, his beard resting on his round belly, snorts in derision. "There are always tales from the hills. Wolves, most like. Bandits, possibly. Whenever someone's careless or unlucky we start hearing about kakodaimones, but if you pay attention and don't shirk your offerings, the gods tend to watch over you. Young folks today, born without stones, they are." He takes a deep swig from the wineskin, belches, and passes it along.

Across the fire sits a tall thin man twisting his

hands in folds of his festival khiton. "All very well to scoff when you haven't stirred from your home fire all winter. I've not only heard the tales and listened to the wailing of women whose small ones have gone missing, I heard the sounds myself, not ten nights back, coming up from the lowlands and seeking a bed for the night. There was a crescent moon, and the twilight was near done, and I was making my way up near the stream that flows east from the Ladon. I stopped to rest, and while sitting on a boulder on the knees of that mountain shaped like a wolf fang I heard footfalls. Not a man; something four-footed, and big. I stayed quiet. I have my knife and a slingshot, but taking down a bear or wolf at night is a skill that might daunt a better hunter than I. The footsteps stopped at the tree line, but the silence that fell was not an easy one, and you may sniff at me, but I felt my lads creep up inside me. I was trembling like a maiden when the reavers come."

The older man raises a furry eyebrow. "Some men aren't made for the life of a bard. If footsteps in a forest are enough to turn you woman, find a weavers' group. Our hills are wild, and while more than creatures wander them, they rarely bother a man who knows both his prayers and his weaponry."

The thin man's brows draw together. "I haven't finished my tale. Nor am I a coward. I have fought with Mentor's outfit against the sea raiders, and I know how to handle spear and shield. But this was no bandit or soldier, I tell you, nor was it bear or boar. I could feel eyes on me, and I could feel them take my measure. And more: there was a coldness to that thing out there. It almost seemed as if it were—I don't know—maybe amused by my terror. I could see a glint of green, as if those eyes were blinking at me while they contemplated my fate. So I prayed, brothers, and I prayed aloud and hard. And I'm not ashamed to say that while I prayed, I grew so afraid that I called upon my Mam, gone these twelve years. And now that I think back on it, it was then that the thing in the trees left off staring at me like I was a piece of bread and honey, and I heard the footfalls move off. And it weren't until they'd been gone and quiet for a long stretch of time—I know not just how long—that I heard the normal sounds of the night return."

A squat drummer with a bushy shock of black wiry hair lets out a yelp of laughter. "And did you also piss your breeches like a baby? Call for your Mam? What man would even admit to doing any such thing?"

It is Hyakinthos who speaks into the firelit quiet that follows the round of guffaws. "A man who is sharing something true, perhaps. Not many would have the courage to tell that tale to a band of ruffians like you. And it sounds not unlike some stories I've heard on my rounds as well. Doors are closed and barred at night, and a simple singer who doesn't find shelter before the sun sets will not find the hospitality he once did. I thank you, friend, for being brave enough to share your story."

The thin man stands abruptly. "In that vein, I'm off to seek shelter for the night. Hopefully the festival atmosphere of xenia will prevail somewhere, even if not here in our bardic circle." He stalks off like a heron.

The man who had been speaking as Lykeion arrived shakes his head. "That was ill done, lads. I know that man, and he's a stout fellow. All of us walk the night paths and know how to handle ourselves, so when one of us says there's danger in the night, it's a foolish man who laughs it off. I tell you, there's something in these hills, and it's more trouble than we've seen in our lifetimes." He stands, taking his pipes and the almost empty wineskin. "I'm for my bed. There's a group of fisher folk who have offered me food and protection in return for my tales as they head back to the shore. If you don't have a place staked out, I suggest you stick together. And stay by the fire."

Raising a hand, he disappears into the night.

Another man, a stranger to the group of musicians, speaks up as if dragging the words from dark water. "I heard a tale around the dark of the moon, so ghastly I gave it little credence. But with such things occurring to men not given to fancies, there may be more to it than I want to believe."

The black-haired drummer squints into firelight, then raises his bushy brows in the stranger's direction.

"Go on, then. If nothing else, a scary story may well inspire a song."

The man does not smile. "If you had seen the faces of the men who told me, you would not blithely talk of songs. The tale has haunted my dreams, and I do not wish to remember it or tell it, but I think it needs telling."

He stirs on his seat, and his voice takes on the rhythm and tenor of a trained bard.

"In the highlands of Akhaia I met a family performing burial rites over a girl. I have never seen such grim faces. They threatened me with angry words, but when I persuaded them of my integrity, they told me what had occurred.

"Some days before, the daughter of the family, a maiden of ten or eleven years, began to speak of visions of wonder. She talked of cups of gold, clouds with wings, bowls overflowing with honey and milk, daimones of perilous beauty. They dismissed her talk as the fantasies of a silly girl, but one evening as dusk fell, she was seen running as fast as a hind of Artemis along a pathway that led to the mountains. She disappeared into the foothills. Her brother set out to find her, but her speed left him far behind, and he was unable to track her in the gloom. He persevered, however, coming finally to a ghastly waste of broken rock and withered scrub and thorns that tore his legs. There he saw, dimly in the darkness, a horse. It was thin and lame, wasted hindquarters barely as broad as a stick, and there was a body flung across its back. He ran to it, ignoring the injuries to his feet, and dragged the body from the horse. He recognized the shift and scratched legs of his sister. But the body had no head. And as he cried out in horror, the horse turned to him, and he saw that the horse was likewise headless, its neck oozing. He picked up the body of his sister and tried to flee, but the horse came after him and knocked him down among the rocks, rearing and kicking at him with jagged hooves.

"As he tried to escape among the boulders and scrub, dragging the body of the girl after him, she too jerked into a semblance of life and fought him, tearing at him with nails and kicking as hard as the horse.

"The boy battled both of them valiantly until rosy-fingered Dawn cast veils of gray into the east. He was finally able to stab the horse between the ribs with a sharp stick, causing dark blood to gush, and it retreated. His last glimpse of it was worse than any part of the battle, for it rendered down, like fat in a fire, and became a mass of darkness, which slithered away among the stones, leaving a viscous trail which clung to his feet.

"I saw his feet. They were blackened as if he had been barefoot in a blizzard. He is lame now, and silent.

"When the thing left, the body of the girl collapsed and became as any other dead thing.

"They burned her, and buried the ashes. They did not find her head."

The group of musicians falls silent.

The moon is journeying westward, the stars fainting before it, but Lykeion finds he is not tired, nor inclined to unroll his blankets with the musicians left by the fire, who are beginning to snore. He shoulders his pack, wraps his cloak around himself, unstrings his lyre, and begins to follow the track of the moon, no destination in mind, just walking, and pondering the things he has heard in the course of the festival. But despite the shiver of alarm planted in his head by the bards' reports, he finds that his mind will not dwell on the troubling tales. It keeps returning to the slender figure before Artemis' shrine, and how the waves of her hair fell before her face, and how she did not giggle or glance his way, and how her back curved like his lyre from her shoulders. He wonders what color her hair is when not drained of all hues by moonlight. He imagines what her voice sounds like. He plays with different things he could have said, clever things, that might have made her laugh, and look up at him with those wide eyes full of admiration instead of indifference. He considers scenarios in which he came up with the perfect thing to say that would have stopped her from leaving him alone before the shrine, something witty perhaps, or better yet, something wise, as she did not have the air of a frivolous girl. He is picturing her so vividly that when he sees her climbing the hill before him, her willowy form clearly delineated in the bright moonlight, for a moment he is not even surprised.

She is disappearing over the crest of the hill, almost half a mile ahead of him, when he comes to himself. He almost shouts out to her, but catches himself. A girl walking alone at night in the mountains is unlikely to respond joyfully to a stranger yelling from behind her on the trail. Instead, trying not to make more noise than necessary and alarming her, he quickens his pace and hopes to close the distance between them before alerting her to his presence. He can only hope it will be a pleasant surprise for her, and starts wracking his brain as he climbs for something to say to her that will not make him sound like a rustic dolt.

As he crests the hill, just a few minutes after her, he sees that she has left the faint pathway and is making her way to a hut, sheltered under an outcropping of stone. A few stately pines grow nearby, casting spiky shadows across the yard where the girl is approaching the doorway. Lykeion is ecstatic. Xenia, the ancient law of hospitality, will likely allow him to sleep not only under a roof this night, but near this girl, and give him a chance to make a better impression on her.

But before the girl can reach the shadowed

entranceway, the door is flung open and a woman rushes out. She stops dead a few paces from the girl.

"Kiri!" she cries out. "Did you see the babies? Gods above and below, tell me you know where the babies are!" The woman bursts into fierce sobs.

The girl rushes forward and grabs the woman by the arms. Lykeion can hear her talking urgently but cannot make out the words. The paralysis brought on by the woman's cry falls from him, and he begins to run toward them. At the sound of his rapid footsteps they both turn to face him. The woman thrusts the girl behind her and stands with her hands outstretched as if to ward him off. But the girl twists out from behind, and crouches tautly, ready to spring. Lykeion is shocked to see a slender knife glint bright in the moonlight, and slides clumsily to a halt ten paces from the women, on the patch of earth before their home.

"No, no, I'm not here to hurt you, I heard the cry and came to help." His words tumble over each other, his breath coming in gasps, his hands like the older woman's stretched before him, trying to demonstrate a lack of threat even if his voice cannot. The girl does not move. The slash of silver is rock-steady in her hand, and her eyes do not blink. Lykeion tries again. "I saw you earlier, at the Mounykhia gathering. I saw you offer the amphiphontes. I saw you walking before me up the mountain and hoped to speak to you, maybe to ask for a night's shelter. I'm a bard. I would never hurt you."

But before the girl can reply, the older woman's voice shrills, cracking with hysteria. "Where is my son? What have you done with my little boy?"

Finally the tall girl removes her intense focus from Lykeion, turning shocked eyes on the woman.

"Mother, what are you saying?"

"Patrokles is gone! So is Kephalos's and Eleni's baby! Something has taken our children!"

Chapter 4

MISSING

A PAIR OF HAWKS DANCES A COMPLEX DUET OF lazy circles, high in the mild afternoon sky. Small clouds dance with them, pirouetting, separating, re-forming, bright white and cheerful, spring celebrants. A small brown rabbit is flat and motionless near a stand of young ash trees. It quivers when the cries of the hawks float down, or their shadows brush the grass.

Two women guard a herd of goats not far from the crouching rabbit. New grass ripples at their feet, a playful breeze tugs at their hair, but they do not sing, or play with the baby goats, or speak to each other. They sit on the same large boulder but they do not look at each other.

The sun is sinking when a trio of figures trudges

⟨er the hill and down the meadow toward the goats and their keepers. The younger woman leaps to her feet, but halts when she sees the weary attitude of the newcomers, and her shoulders slump.

"Eleni. They're back."

The older woman lifts a small, wan face briefly, then disappears again behind a tangle of colorless hair. She says nothing.

The girl waits, fingernails digging painful crescents in her palms. But the face of the big man who reaches her first answers all her questions. Stephanos touches her cheek, lines of weariness graven deeply around his mouth. Her eyes meet his, and he shakes his head slowly.

"Nothing, Kiri. We found nothing."

The youngest of the three men steps out from behind the others, straightening his shoulders.

"Not nothing, Stephanos. Tales of loss, from every quarter. We are not the only ones to lose children. Something is stalking these hills and valleys."

The third man snarls, "And what loss is yours? I know of no family you have lost, lyre-plucker." The sneer is belied by the desperation in his eyes.

Stephanos's deep voice is gentle. "Kephalos. The bard is here to help. Don't vent your anger on him."

Kephalos does not answer. As he turns to the slight form of the silent woman, his voice catches in a sob. "We will find her, Eleni. I swear before the Gods we will." He raises a clenched fist. "On the bones of my ancestors, I swear it. By blood and blade…."

"Kephalos!" gasps Kiri. "You mustn't! Do not swear oaths you might not keep!"

Kephalos gathers the unresisting form of his wife to him, doubling over as if he has taken a punch to the gut. "If I break the oath, what of it? If we do not find our daughter, the kakodaimones can take me."

But he does not finish the oath.

"Where is Mother?" asks Kiri, unable to look at the couple huddled under the boulder, frozen in their grief.

"She took Karissa back to the hut. The little one was exhausted. She's preparing a meal for us. Let's go. We don't want to be out on the mountain when darkness falls." Stephanos sighs, looks out over the goats scattered throughout the meadow, and gives a piercing whistle. Three large dogs leap from their invisible vantage points in the grass and begin to round up the goats.

Goats, dogs and humans trudge through the red sunset.

A curl of fragrant smoke wafts from inside the small hut nestled against the mountain's hip. While the men pen the goats, Kiri and Eleni step inside to find Aglaia wearily boiling roots in the cauldron, tempering their toughness with herbs and some shreds of dried goat meat, a sprinkling of precious sea salt. Little Karissa is wound into a ball on a pile of skins in the corner, so deeply asleep that not even the smell of hot food rouses her. Kiri touches her mother's arm. Aglaia pauses for a brief moment, but does not speak nor look at her older daughter. Kiri drops her hand. She turns to the motionless figure of Eleni huddled near the door and draws her closer to the fire.

The group eats in silence.

As Kiri begins to clear the bowls, a sob escapes Aglaia. "I hope Patrokles gets something to eat tonight." She sinks to the floor, face covered, shoulders shaking. Stephanos enfolds her in his big arms. Karissa stirs and moans. Kiri goes to her. She picks her up, hushing her, and carries her to fire where she dips a hard loaf end into the bit of stew remaining at the bottom of the pot and feeds the little girl as if she were a baby. She looks up at the others.

"What happened today?"

The older men do not move or speak. Both stare heavily into the fire. Aglaia lifts her head with an effort, but when her eyes touch her daughter's she winces and looks away. Lips tightening, Kiri turns to the young bard sitting diffidently by the door.

"Lykeion. Tell me."

He glances at the other men, who remain motionless and silent. Then, looking at Kiri's scowl, he squares his shoulders and instinctively reaches for his lyre, then drops his hand sheepishly.

Kephalos draws Eleni's slight form more closely to

his side. "Eleni doesn't need to hear this. We'll retire."

But Eleni pulls sharply away from him. "I will hear," she says. Her soft voice has an undertone of iron. Kephalos starts to protest, but subsides when she stares at him, lips pressed in a thin line. "Speak on, bard."

Lykeion meets Kiri's uncompromising eyes, wets his lips and begins.

"We met a group of traders making their way inland from Elis at great speed, carrying almost no merchandise. We shared food and fire with them on the bank of the Erymanthos, and heard their tale. They did not experience these events personally, but spoke to the sailors who did.

"A trade ship was heading north from Lakonia with a cargo of wine, oil and a few trained warhorses. They came inland to replenish their fresh water supplies at a river mouth, and were setting out again around dusk when they heard loud moaning coming from a small cove near a region of sea-caves. Thinking there may have been a wrecked ship in need of rescue (or plunder, who knows?), they rowed into the shallow waters and called out. But as the nose of their boat nudged the soft sand, there came a scrabbling at the sides, and a terrible stench. As the sailors crowded to see what was assailing their vessel, there came swarming onto the deck a crowd of small forms. They were children. They were rotting. Their flesh was sliding from their bones,

and their teeth gleamed. They shambled toward the sailors, crying and moaning, sobbing that they had come to find Amphitrite, but She refused to be their Mother. The children fell upon the sailors, gnawing and ripping. They were slow, and weak, and easy to dismember, but they were desperate and many. The ship was stuck in the sand, and no man could free himself from the fight against the children to dislodge it.

"The battle should have been over in minutes, but the sailors say it took all night. It was not until dawn began to steal over the sea that they were able to beat back the still-shambling dead children, who sank like stones as they were shoved from the ship. Finally they floated free with the tide. They found that three of their number had been torn to pieces and partially devoured. They performed the rites, and consigned the bodies of their mates to the sea and to Amphitrite's care. And they sailed as fast and far as they could.

"That night as darkness fell over the waters they heard the voices of their dead crewmates, crying from the waves. And the dead men came climbing over the sides of the ship, moaning and begging for their friends to share food with them, that they were starving. Their skins no longer knit closely over their torn organs, and some carried their limbs or their soft inner parts in their arms.

"The crew had to kill their shipmates again, and

scatter the body parts.

"The casks of wine and oil were shattered and lost, and the warhorses went mad and leapt into the sea. The crew made harbor with no further adventures, but every man's hair has turned pure white, and none will venture forth onto the shining surface of Poseidon's realm again."

Kiri stares at him. Karissa begins to whimper. Aglaia takes her from Kiri's unresponsive arms, and lies down with her in a dark corner, cuddling and singing softly to her. Lykeion returns Kiri's wide-eyed gaze. The two older men sit stolidly, staring at the fire.

Eleni's eyes shine wetly in the fading firelight, but her soft jaw remains firm. "Did they describe the children? Did they say how old they were?"

Kephalos replies, "No, Eleni. I asked these same questions. The traders did not know. They did not tolerate our questions. They were angry at not being able to trade their goods, and very afraid of what they heard. They just wanted to get out of the region, and go as quickly as possible to the Attik plain and put this land behind them."

As Eleni's face sinks into her hands, Kephalos catches Lykeion's eye and shakes his head faintly. Stephanos, Lykeion and Kiri sit in silence while Kephalos gently but firmly nudges his wife to their pile of furs, some distance from the fire. Not far from them lie Aglaia and Karissa, twitching and murmuring together in unquiet sleep.

Kiri wets her lips. It takes two tries before she can choke out words. "Is there more?"

Lykeion closes his eyes briefly, then meets hers once more. "Yes," he says softly.

"Tell me."

Stephanos rises abruptly. "I'll go check on the flocks." He steps outside, silent for such a big man.

Lykeion eyes Kiri. "It is not a story I re-tell willingly, and there are few tales indeed about which I can say that."

"You will tell me," she says, her voice soft as a breath, but adamant. She turns from him and adds more wood to the fire.

Lykeion sighs. "Not far from where the Mounykhia took place is a small community of herders, like you. We met them only a day after we set out, and had they not recognized my voice from the festival, they may have killed us in their fury and fear.

"They pasture their goats on Wolf Fang Mountain, below the sharp peaks on the verdant upland meadows. One night, not even a half a moon ago, they heard howls, and ran out to their herds only to find the goatherd lying insensible, the dogs gone, and half their goats torn apart. The goatherd survived but could tell them nothing, so they assumed that wolves had attacked, and prepared to hunt them down. But they found no tracks, nor any sign of other predators like bears or cats. They were about to turn home in frustration when they saw a foxfire, gleaming in the darkness of the woods. They followed it under the trees. It flickered and danced, and led them deeper, until under the light of the late-rising moon they saw a fox, a large red one, sitting in a circle of huge white mushrooms.

"It had a severed human hand in its mouth.

"When it saw them it trotted out of the nymph circle, and led them on, often turning and waiting for them. They followed it until daybreak, when it led them to a stream. Lying half in the water was the body of a young woman, dreadfully mutilated, and signs of a terrible struggle all around. The mud and reeds at the bank of the stream were crushed and mangled. Blood and torn clothing littered the ground. They searched the area, looking for whatever could have perpetrated such an atrocity, and they found the body of a man nearby, leaning against a tree. He was still alive. His limbs had been severed from his body and were lying nearby, except for his missing hand. They asked him what had happened, but he could not say. His tongue had been torn from his mouth. His eyes implored them, but he could not tell his tale.

"He died shortly thereafter. The hunters performed the rites over the bodies, and burned them. They returned to their families, and stand guard turn and turn about, not traveling nor welcoming strangers.

They believe they are being watched at night, and do not venture forth from their fires unless they are at least three, and armed."

Kiri closes her eyes. Lykeion makes an abortive move toward her, but stops himself and settles back, gazing into the now-leaping fire, his mouth set in a grim line.

After a while Stephanos softly enters the hut. "All is quiet. The goats sleep, and the dogs are relaxed. But we need to keep a constant watch. Come relieve me at sunrise."

Kiri looks at her father's shadowed eyes. "You are exhausted, Father. I sat idle in the meadows today, and I will not sleep now after hearing these tales. I will sit with the dogs until sunrise. Sleep, and prepare for tomorrow."

Stephanos's thick brows draw together, but Lykeion stands and forestalls him.

"She's right, Stephanos. I'll stand guard with her." Stephanos's scowl deepens, and the young man adds hastily, "I swear before the Shining Ones of Olympos that I will offer no outrage or forward behavior to your daughter. I am here to help."

Kiri's mouth quirks in an unwilling smile. "And I have my knife, Father, which you yourself taught me to use. Whatever endangers me in the night, it won't be this bard."

Lykeion's throat moves convulsively.

"Very well," says Stephanos eventually. "Stay by the pen, and take a torch. Wolves fear the fire."

But "No," says Kiri firmly. "The torch ruins my night sight, and whatever stalks these hills does not fear what mere beasts fear. I can see well in the dark, and if I don't like what I see, I will call for you, Father. The darkness itself has never frightened me, and what it holds now will not be thwarted by our little torches."

Stephanos looks at Lykeion. Lykeion gives a helpless little shrug.

"I can yell as loudly as she," Lykeion offers.

Stephanos snorts, and turns away.

The goats murmur happily as Kiri leans over the woven-twig fence, and the pure black doe butts her affectionately. Kiri rubs the knobby silken head for a moment, then settles on a slight mound. Eyes gleam red in the grass where the biggest herd dog crouches nearby, panting slightly. Lykeion comes and stands in front of her.

"Shouldn't we move to the trees where there's shelter?"

Kiri eyes him. After a long moment she replies, "No. Shelter means that I can't see what's coming at me. If I'm in the open I'm visible, but I can also see all around, and so can the dogs." She sighs. "Whatever is stalking these regions won't be deterred easily. All we can hope for is to see something coming in time to alert the others, and that our numbers will save us."

He sits down close to her, but not too close. He has not forgotten the panther stance when he came upon her too quickly in darkness, just a handful of nights before.

"Do you really think that would be enough to save us?" he asks quietly.

Kiri is silent for several minutes. When she speaks, her voice is so low that he has to strain to hear her above the small night noises, and the mutterings of the goats nearby. "I think I know what's happening. No. That's not it, I don't know, not really. But I saw something, last spring. And then something else—as winter was ending, right after Eleni's baby…." She chokes, then continues, "After Eleni's baby was born. And I think the—the things I have seen are connected to what's going on. To the deaths. And the missing children." She swallows audibly. "I think I have to go find Her. And ask Her to stop it."

Lykeion stares at her, dumbfounded. "Go where? Ask who? Ask what?"

Kiri's eyes gleam in the starlight before she squeezes them tightly shut. "I think there's a Goddess in a cave. And I think She's very, very angry."

Chapter 5

THINGS SEEN

KIRI SIGHS AND SHIFTS THE PACK AGAIN, TRYING to ease the ache in her shoulders. The sun is hovering above the line of western hills. It is bright and hot, and she is tired. They have been walking for several days without any clear destination or goal. The pressure is building like a looming thunderhead.

"Let me retie that for you," says Lykeion, reaching for one of the straps binding her pack to her back, but she slaps his hand away crossly.

"Leave it. I'll fix it when we stop."

"You're heaving and sighing like a seal. If it's uncomfortable, it's stupid not to fix it. Or do you like heaving and sighing?"

"I'd like to make some progress without finding excuses to stop every time a cloud passes over the sun's face. What's stupid is wandering along like we're on a picnic. Or do you like dawdling like a broody sheep?"

"We're wandering because you say there's a cave we have to find, but you don't know where, or how far, or what direction, or what we're going to find when we get there. Maybe if you tell me just what it is you've got us out here seeking we could actually march along with some purpose instead of all this girlish vagueness."

Kiri whirls and glares at him. He stands his ground and glares back. After a moment she sighs again and drops her gaze.

"I know I'm being vague. I'm sorry. But it's not something I can easily explain. You heard what I told my parents. I'm not trying to keep you in the dark, it's just so hard to put into words."

Lykeion does not stop glaring at her. "I'm a bard. I work with words. You could try, and if it's not clear, you could keep trying. You're worse than a mumbling mantis breathing sacred smoke and talking gibberish. At least a diviner wouldn't have me stalking the hills when danger is afoot, and slapping me for trying to be of help."

Kiri's mouth twitches. "Words don't fix everything. And sometimes you can use a good slap."

His gaze finally relaxes, and he almost smiles. "So can you. But I'm too scared of your father to do it, even if you deserve it."

Her face hardens again. "Deserve or no, I don't need my father to keep me safe from the likes of you."

"Your father sent me out here with you to keep you safe from worse than me," he shoots back. "And if it hadn't been for me, you wouldn't have been allowed to make this crazy trek. So you can quit threatening me with fists or knives, okay?"

Her sudden grin takes his breath away. "Okay." She turns from him, and begins trudging up the rocky hillside again, pebbles skittering away from her goat-skin boots.

The dusk has dissolved into damp darkness when they finally halt, making their simple camp by star-light. They have not encountered any game that day, and make their meal of hard waybread baked with fat and a little meat. Lykeion mixes water into wine in a bowl and hands it to Kiri as she sits back with a sigh into her blankets.

"Tell me again why we're not searching the mountains near Kephalos and Eleni's cave. Isn't that where you encountered this….situation? I don't understand why you feel we shouldn't start at the beginning."

Lykeion cannot see her face in the dark, but her voice betrays her uncertainty. "I've been up that mountain a hundred times since then, and many hundreds more before. I tell you, the path that led me into the mountain cave isn't there. I've looked for it. Wherever that cave is, it's not something you can get to the same way you find other places. But I'm sure I can find it again. I'm sure She'll let me. At least, I think so." Her voice quavers. "I don't know what else to do. We've got to find Her."

He sits in silence for a few minutes. Then, "Kiri, I believe you. But I don't think this is going to work. We've got to make a better plan. We can't just wander around and hope that a Goddess whose name we don't even know will guide us in. It's not just the danger out here, although the Gods know that's enough to daunt a mighty warrior let alone a bard and goatherd. But the more time that passes, the less likely we are to find any of the children alive, if indeed there's any hope of it now. And your people are terrified for you. We can't keep them waiting forever for word, even if it's bad news."

The silence from across the little fire goes on for so long that he wonders if she has fallen asleep. Then she sets the wine bowl down with a decisive thump. Her voice is firm and cool.

"I don't know how I know, Lykeion, but this is what I have to do. I'll walk until She's ready to bring me to Her. And if She doesn't—well, I'll go home. But there's no strategy to lay out, and nothing else to be done. Just keep walking in the mountains." An edge creeps into her voice. "You don't have to come with me. Go make a plan, and see how well it works."

Fire leaps into Lykeion's face, and a hot reply gets caught behind his teeth. He wrestles it down his gullet, turns from the fire without another word and pulls his blankets over him. The fire dies down to a moody glow, and soon the only sound is steady breathing.

The stars wheel overhead.

Rhythmic thudding makes the ground under the thin blankets jump. Without volition Kiri and Lykeion stretch their hands to each other and clasp them over the now-cool ashes. They do not look through the darkness at each other. Their eyes strain to pierce the cool night air, as the hammerblows continue to fall, louder and louder. A cold breeze picks up, damp and smelling of salt, disturbing in the arid mountains. Kiri's hair blows across her face and clings in sticky strings. Lykeion feels his stomach begin to churn.

A deeper blackness bulks against the sky to the southwest, blotting out the stars. A ragged mane lifts on the wet wind. A pair of green eyes gleam. A terrible trumpet rings out, and the black stallion rears, front hooves raking the stars out of the sky and scattering them into dust. Kiri and Lykeion let go each other's hands to clap them over their own ears. The huge shape steps closer to them, then halts and lowers its triangular head, ears flat against the thick neck. The eyes bore into them. Just as Kiri is about to scream from the pressure of the gaze, the stallion breaks the connection, and turns away, hindquarters like moving boulders, hooves the size of the round shields of mountain archers slamming into the earth as it moves back the way it came. But before it disappears over the ridge, it turns back once more, glaring. Its nostrils flare into a snort so loud it hurts their heads.

And then it is gone. The next thing they know they are stirring in the dawnlight, their bleary eyes blinking at the scattered white ash of the fire.

Lykeion lifts his gaze to meet Kiri's, wincing at the exhausted red-rimmed look of her. He reaches for her, then realizes that they are too far apart to touch.

"Wait—how did we....?" he falters, and falls to silence.

"It was a dream," she whispers back.

"No. It can't have been. You remember it too, I can see you do. We can't have had the same dream."

"It was a dream," she insists, her voice rising. "But it was a true dream."

He stares at her. "You've seen it before. That thing. That horse. Was it a horse?"

Her glassy gaze falters and drops. "Yes," she whispers. "Yes, I've seen him before. I don't know what he is, but I'm so afraid of him." She looks up again, and her tired eyes lock onto his. "This is what I've been looking for. We have to follow him."

He stares at her, aghast. "Follow him? That nightmare beast that just wrecked any future prospects for peaceful sleep in this lifetime! Are you mad?"

Her long, tangled hair hides her face. "No. Maybe." With a deep, shuddering sigh that wracks Lykeion's heart she pushes her hair back, then hauls herself to her feet, giving him a disconcerting glimpse of what she will look like as an old woman. "I have enough mint and marjoram to make us some tea, and there's a little bread left. We should make a point of hunting, and gathering more herbs as we go. Will you stir up the fire?"

And that is how Lykeion finds himself a short while later, his belly warmed with the light breakfast, following Kiri over the crest of the mountain, and down toward the plain below, heading southwest.

It is four days later when Lykeion and Kiri crest a particularly challenging ridge to find the ground falling away under their feet. A shining slab of gleaming, shimmering light spreads before them, far away to the barely discernible horizon. Kiri's breath catches in her throat. Words desert her.

Lykeion feels her wonder without tearing his eyes from the moving humps and valleys of green, deep blue and cloud-white. "Io, Poseidon," he breathes, and a seagull screams overhead.

"Is it—it must be the sea," whispers Kiri. "I didn't

know…."

"Yes," he whispers back, not knowing why he whispers. "I've seen it before. But never from a vantage this high. I didn't know it was so vast."

They stand for a time that seems endless, and like no time at all. The afternoon sun ducks behind an errant cloud. The undulating cloak goes dark and forbidding. Kiri shivers.

"It's wonderful. But it terrifies me. Why are we here?"

Lykeion smiles at her. "Because you said we needed to be here. Now what?"

She watches the sea below as the sun slides back into the blue, and the water brightens, seeming to laugh with relief. "We go on, I guess. What else is there?"

Their gazes lock. Then with one accord they begin to pick their way down the crumbling scree, grasping at tough little spiny shrubs as they make their descent toward a tangle of fig, olive, laurel and pine trees that separates the steep hills from the gleaming white crescent where the waves break and murmur.

The fresh breeze that cooled them on the heights becomes tangled in the rocks and stubborn, stunted trees of the slopes. They are both sticky, sweaty, and scratched as they work their way down the last stretch of mountain into the verge of the forest.

Lykeion lands hard on a shelf of stone at the

bottom of the slope, swears briefly, then glances guiltily up the hill behind him with an apology poised on his lips. Before it can fly free, he is knocked off his feet by a hurtling girl who chuffs a surprised "Oof!" then bounces lightly back onto her feet.

"Sorry," she offers, along with her hand. He gazes at it bleakly for a moment before taking it and allowing her to haul him to his feet. He winces as he stands upright, bends over to massage an ankle.

"You're heavier than you look," he tells her, half expecting a sharp reply. But she twinkles at him.

"And you're softer than you look. Are you hurt? Did I do that, or was it that ungraceful shuffle down the last few feet?"

His mouth quirks for a second in spite of himself. "It was steep, and I'm tired. And I wasn't expecting an assault from on high." He tries a tentative step, winces, and sits heavily on a boulder under an olive tree so ancient and gnarled that it hunches over the stone like a crone over a cauldron. "I don't think it's too bad. But I'm going to bind it. Give me a minute."

"I've got it," says Kiri briskly, whipping out a strip of coarsely woven cloth from her pack. A quick practiced glance around the rocky debris at the foot of the hill and the forest stretching to the northeast, and she pounces on a clump of comfrey and some moss from a fallen log. Before he can ask why, she has packed his bruised ankle, wound the strip expertly around it, and tied it firmly into place.

"There you are, my lad. No more lazing! On your feet and let's see if we can make our way to the beach before nightfall. I want to see the ocean up close before the end of the day."

He is working out an appropriately scathing retort when a quavering cry, sodden with inexpressible sorrow, freezes them in place.

The westering sun darkens although no cloud has crossed its face. Without speaking a word they both suddenly remember why they are here, and what they followed to reach this place.

Face gone abruptly ashen, Kiri hands Lykeion his stick and his bundle and helps him to stand. The woods have fallen silent at the cry. Even the insects are hushed. They stand for a moment, the olive branches swaying ever so slightly over their heads. In the silence a rhythmic whisper swells, muted yet somehow enormous, like the soft breathing of a distant dragon.

Eyes wide, Kiri whispers, "What is that? I've never heard anything like that before."

Lykeion replies, "It's the sea. We must be getting close. But that doesn't explain that cry."

Her eyes lift to his. They are swimming with fear. "Oh, Lykeion. What are we doing? This is mad. I don't want to see this. I don't want to know. Let's leave. Let's go home, right now. This was a crazy idea. Let's get out of here."

His hand comes up, almost without volition, and cups her face. He watches a teardrop tremble on her lower lashes, caught like a dewdrop on a spider web, shimmering prisms of color.

"We can't stop now." His fingers move a little, feeling her swallow. "You know we can't turn back now."

The tears shimmer unshed in her eyes. The fear is still there. But her jaw firms under his fingers. She takes a deep breath, and her hand covers his, squeezes.

"No. Of course not." Her gaze shifts into the woods. "Which way?"

He turns slowly, eyes searching the trees. "I don't know. I don't know where that sound came from. It seemed to come from everywhere and nowhere. From the earth itself."

Kiri stands silent, her wide eyes never leaving his face. He takes a deep breath and closes his eyes. At first he feels nothing. Then softly, insidiously, he feels a tug in his mind, a very small tug, like a shoot unfurling in the sun. Barely breathing, he allows his head to orient on the subtle signal, and as he moves the feeling strengthens. He opens his eyes into the red sun. "This way."

They move through the trees. The foliage is too thin to dim the dying daylight, but it seems already dusk. Roots rise suddenly to catch even a carefully placed footfall. Twigs twine and poke, aiming for eyes. Kiri cries out as a branch like a tiny talon draws blood from her cheek, but she stifles the sound as soon as it leaves her lips. It seems to make the trees, formerly familiar and friendly, turn toward them with a terrible eagerness.

"Are you sure?" Kiri whispers, and her hand creeps into his.

"Yes," he whispers back, warmed despite his fear. It is the first time she has spontaneously touched him. His fingers close on her cold ones, and they both feel momentarily braver.

The woodwalk seems to take hours, or days, but beyond the veil of gloom draping the branches they can still see fire in the sky. At the same moment they realize that the dragon breathing has become louder, insistent. Lykeion glances at the orange and purple beyond the treetops and catches himself wondering wearily if there actually is a dragon dozing outside the bounds of the woods, preparing to stretch and yawn and unfurl enormous wings before launching into the starry sky, perhaps with its belly warmed by two young humans. Then he feels Kiri's tug on his hand and halts, dismayed, gazing with her at the hopeless mat of thick gray spidersilk blocking the faint path through the trees.

The mass of strands is not still. It quivers and thrums ceaselessly in the dim light as countless leggy figures, some tiny, some as big as his hand, explore and hunt and build and tear down and reconstruct and wrap and feed. His skin crawls. His hair seems to creep and skitter across his scalp. He can feel Kiri begin to tremble violently.

"Lykeion, I don't think we could get through that in broad daylight let alone now with the night so close upon us." Her voice shivers with despair.

He looks at her. "Can we really go back? Or camp here tonight, and try in the morning?" He shudders at the prospect of sleeping under the night gaze of the hungry trees and the almost subliminal rustling of the webs. He sees his feelings mirrored in her face, her teeth worrying her lower lip as she looks at the silvery glint of the silk before them.

But before she can answer the terrible wavering cry comes again, filling the deep red air, shattering on the sharp branches and drifting down on them like dust. The anguish is unbearable. It lingers long after the sound itself has died away into a trail of soft sobs. The boughs seem drenched in a dew of despair.

Lykeion feels his knees soften. He stiffens them with an effort. Kiri's hands are clenched over her mouth, eyes like moons above them. A tiny sound, a kitten's growl, escapes from behind those hands. Moving convulsively she takes her cloak and wraps it tightly around her head and shoulders, leaving only a slit for her eyes. Taking her knife from her pack, she steps forward and begins to slice and hack her way through the skein of silk, spiders raining on and over her.

Lykeion chokes out a prayer, to whom he cannot say. He follows her.

The last flares of the sunset still inflame the sky when they emerge from the woods, clothes torn, feet bruised, festooned in ragged silk, countless painful lumps rising all over their faces and bodies, scuttling shapes adorning their clothes and hair. The west throbs incarnadine over a jagged arête which falls down into a shadowy bowl.

Down there small horrors are moving.

Kiri steps to the rim of the steep hillside. Below her to the left deep mauve waves break onto the sand, exploding into white foam. She has dreamed her whole life of experiencing her first glimpse of the sea, but neither its majestic roll nor the dragon's breath roar make the slightest impression on her as she stares below her where scores of figures totter on the grass. Even as she watches, some fall and lie motionless.

They have the bodies of children. But they have the heads of horses.

Chapter 6

ON THE BEACH

THE THICK DARK THAT PRECEDES THE DAWN presses down on the two inert forms crumpled together on the crest of the hill above the sea. A wolverine, grinning and hungry, pads close to them, ears lifting. He pauses, sniffs, freezes in place, then hurries away.

There is no further movement on the hill other than the faint breathing of the pair. Not until the eastern horizon pearls ever so faintly and a light cold breeze stirs the girl's matted hair do they stir.

Lykeion comes to consciousness first. He stifles a groan, but the sound is enough to rouse Kiri. Her eyelids flutter, then fly open, freeing the terror that was trapped behind them. Before she can shatter the pre-dawn stillness with her scream he wraps his cloak around them both.

"Hush! We're alive. Be still."

He can see the effort it takes for her to wrestle the panic back down her throat. After a moment she croaks, "It was real. What we saw. The—the children." She shudders convulsively and looks around. "How did we get here?"

"I don't know. We saw that—those things. I don't remember anything else until I woke up here, just now."

The distant murmur of the ocean rolls in their ears. A glimmering line spreads in the east, separating the sea from the black sky. It is too dark for Lykeion to make out Kiri's face but he can feel the waves of agony rolling over her.

"Lykeion. Patrokles was there."

His words stick in his throat. He has to swallow several times before he can force them out. "How could you tell?"

She drops her face into her hands. He can feel her shoulders shaking although she makes no sound. Finally she lifts her head and says thickly, "I know him. Even without—his face. I know him. It was my brother." Her voice stumbles to a halt. Then, on a rising note of horror, "He was trying to carry a baby. It was Eleni's baby. She was too heavy for him. He's so small, almost a baby himself, but he was trying to take care of Eleni's...." She begins to sob violently, furiously.

Lykeion is at a loss. He is so stunned by her words, after the unreality of the past evening, that he cannot even reach a comforting hand to her.

Suddenly she stops crying mid-sob and flings herself to her feet, tears flying from her face and hitting Lykeion like tiny blows.

"I'm going back. I'm going to get Patrokles. I'm going to take him and Eleni's baby out of there." She whirls, dark against the still-starred sky, and grabs her pack. "I'm going to get them all."

Lykeion gapes at her as she spins her cloak over her shoulders and strides off. A protest flutters in his throat, then he leaps up and runs after her.

They do not go back down the hill and into the woods. Without exchanging a word they head north, staying on the crest of the high ground, keeping the sea in sight. The eastern sky turns gold, then green and rose. As the sun slides smoothly up, they reach the edge of the bowl and stare down.

Lykeion half expects to see nothing. Perhaps the nightmare scene was part of the same hallucination as the gargantuan stallion who had led them there. Maybe the fear and exhaustion of their long trek culminating in the colony of spiders had overwhelmed their senses. Probably the beach below was inhabited by fisherfolk, or a herd of deer, or nothing at all.

But what moves on the grassy meadow near the

beach are not things that a rational man can accept.

Children stagger through the short tough grass. Some lie together in forlorn heaps. The horse heads nod and sag on necks too thin to support them. A few of the bigger ones are on hands and knees, trying miserably to graze.

Guttural noises drift up on the bright morning air.

On the beach the waves are rolling in. There are forms in the white foam of the gentle breakers. To Lykeion's astonished eyes they almost seem to be girls, lithe maidens with flowing hair and limbs of pearl. Armfuls of soft seaweeds, alive with small silver fish, are thrown onto the wet sand. Crabs busily haul it across the beach, depositing the glistening cargo onto the grass of the meadow.

Some of the grotesqueries are trying to nibble on it. The fishes flop, then lie still.

Where the woods meet the meadow there is a small band of wild mares, a few grazing but most huddled together, stamping, restless.

"Where is he?" breathes Kiri, eyes searching the impossible scene. Lykeion sees a small boy leaning exhaustedly against a boulder by the sand. He points. The boy is pulling strands of the seaweed free and bringing them one by one to his small muzzle. At his feet lies an infant girl, her tiny filly head moving fitfully. A crab scuttles up to her, clutching a tiny silver fish in its claws, and seems to offer it to her, but she ignores it. It drops the fish at the boy's feet and hurries back to the waterline.

"Patrokles!" Kiri leaps forward, then freezes.

"Little doula. Still braver than you are wise, I see." The voice is rich, melodic, rippling with a hint of humor that causes the hair on the back of Lykeion's neck to spring erect. They both spin around so quickly that Kiri falls into Lykeion and they almost go down in a heap, but he grabs her. They find their feet and stare open-mouthed at the figure which has come up behind them.

Lykeion battles back a shout of fear when he sees the great dark stallion before them. But even as his body twitches in terror he realizes that this is not the massive beast they had seen before.

It is indeed a black stallion, but where the other one bulged with rock-like muscle, this one is lean, lithe, and long of limb. The mane and tail are as green as the dawn sky before the sun rises, and so are the eyes that peer at them from under the silky forelock. Those eyes gleam with amusement.

Kiri's jaw falls open. "It's you. The foal. The foal from the cave. Out of the dark mare. You spoke then too."

The elegant head dips in an ironic bow. "Of course, little doula. I could never forget the girl who helped my mother bring me into the world. And I didn't think it likely that you would forget me.

I am Areion." The lips stretch into an unsettling smile. "And of course you also remember my sister."

Kiri cries out, "The baby with the horse's head."

The stallion again dips his head, a parody of courtesy. "Which brings us to our present circumstance."

Lykeion brings a hand to his head. "I don't understand. How is it that you can speak?"

The green eyes rest on his face for a moment, then dismiss him and turn back to the girl. She is poised on her toes as if ready to run.

"You cannot go to them. No," as she moves convulsively. "If you truly wish to help the victims of my sister's rage you will listen to me. For I will give you the only hope you have, and I assure you it is a slender hope indeed."

Kiri swallows hard, but meets his eyes with a direct gaze. The green eyes blink. "I will hear you. And I will do whatever I have to, to free my brother. To free them all. I will not leave these children here. I will not leave without them."

Leaf-shaped ears swivel back, then flick forward, tips almost touching. "You will. For if you approach them in that place, they will all die. My sire is displeased at the violation of order and keeps them in a state of prolonged existence while a solution is sought. But intrusion by a mortal is not permissible. You are fortunate to have survived the very sight. Indeed, had I not intervened on your behalf, you would surely now be standing before the throne of the All-Receiver."

Lykeion feels Kiri stiffen, then slump beside him. A fierce sob tears from her, then she tosses back her matted hair and steps toward the horse, fists clenched. "I don't believe you. I must go to them."

Lykeion puts a hand on her rigid arm, looking at the stallion. "You said a solution is being sought. What do you mean?"

The stallion shakes his forelock from his strange eyes and takes a step forward. "Bard, that is the right question to ask. The Mother, Demeter, is enraged, and in her rage she has produced the Daughter Who Must Not Be Named. This daughter is enacting her rage throughout the land. My sister cannot be approached. Do not dream that you can. But maybe—just maybe—our Mother can be. Because she may remember you, girl, there is a slender chance that you might be the one who can appease her.

"I will not lie to you, little doula. The danger is grave beyond your imagining. She is terrible in her wrath. Death is the gentlest outcome most can hope for in her presence. And as you know, far, far worse is possible.

"But my Mother bore me too, and I am not born to bring terror and perversion. If you are willing to face more danger than you ever have in your life, you may be the one human who can help bring order back to the world."

Kiri gapes at him. "Worse danger than I've already faced?"

Lykeion swallows fear like a lump of charcoal in his throat. He puts a hand on Kiri's shoulder, feeling it tremble. "What must we do?" he manages to say around the lump.

The stallion eyes him, measuring. Suddenly he arches his neck, the green mane lifting then settling like a line of seabirds on a wave.

"Go find Pan."

Chapter 7

GO FIND PAN

TRUDGING THROUGH THE FOOTHILLS OF THE Arkadian mountains, Lykeion finally breaks the tense silence.

"Why are you angry with me?" he says to the rigid back ahead of him.

Kiri does not look back. "I am not angry with you."

"Why will you not talk to me?"

"I am thinking."

"I am thinking too. Mayhap if we share our thoughts with each other we can come up with a better plan."

Kiri whirls in the middle of the stony track to face him. "A better plan? A speaking horse and his demonic sister have sent us in search of a god who might kill us on sight, and you want to improve on his plan?

Perhaps put together a battle strategy?" Her eyes blaze. "Or make a song about it?"

A flush rises in Lykeion's face. He bites back the retorts piling up behind his teeth until he is able to swallow them all.

"I will make a song to be sung through the ages if we live through this. But, for now, I am thinking more about finding a river, so I can make the reed pipes Areion said I would need to summon Pan. What do you say to directing our steps that way as we make our way to the mountains?"

"I heard him, too. The Ladon runs down to the plains near my home. That is where we are headed. But every step we take carries us farther and farther from Patrokles and the other children, and I do not think they can live much longer. I am so afraid."

He reaches out to her and takes her hand, expecting her to yank it away. He is surprised and pleased when her fingers curl around his.

She sighs. "From the plain, we can make our way up into the wild country of which Areion spoke. We could stop and tell my parents what is happening, but I do not know what we could say. If they knew the children were alive, nothing would stop them from going after them, and Areion said that would mean their deaths. I am afraid they would try to stop me. To stop us. We have to do this ourselves, and we have to do it soon." She squeezes his hand, drops it, and turns back resolutely to the hike. She shoots him a half-smile over her shoulder. "I am glad you are here. Anyone else would have fled screaming long ago. If they had sense, anyway."

He gives the back of her head a rueful glance. "That would have made a very poor ballad."

That night, as they make their late camp under a lonely, twisted cypress, he says, hesitantly, "Areion is a god, or some sort of divine being. A speaking horse with mane and tail that color could only have sprung from a god. So why does he need us? If he is helping his father bring back the natural order, why doesn't he, himself, deal with his sister? Or appeal to their goddess mother? Why us? And why Pan?"

Kiri has been finger-combing her hair into a long, smooth veil that shimmers faintly in the starlight. She is silent for a few moments as she begins to twist it into a braid.

"I do not know. Perhaps Pan, the god of wild places and things, can control her. And perhaps the gods work through humans at times, at least when it is a matter that involves humans. Since the Daughter Who Must Not Be Named has been taking children and bringing death to the people of the land, maybe we mortals must be the ones to stop her. Or maybe it is simply that I was there at the birth." She smiles wanly. "It is an honor I could have done without."

Lykeion shudders. "I have not seen her, but seeing

those children was enough. It is hard to fathom an anger so great that it would cause that. She must be fury incarnate. The Mistress of Rage."

"Yes," whispers Kiri. "The Despoina. The rage of her mother, let loose upon the world. Somehow, we have to persuade Demeter to let go her anger and to stop her daughter from wreaking destruction."

They do not speak again. Eventually, they sleep.

Around noon the next day, they hear the faint sound of rushing water. A gentle slope studded with golden wildflowers leads down to a line of willows and sycamores. The Ladon sparkles between the moving leaves.

Their tired feet pick up their pace. By the time they reach the trees, they are running. Barely pausing to fling their packs onto the soft earth, they plunge into the water. Kiri shrieks at the cold shock and laughs out loud. Lykeion stares at her, enchanted.

"Your laugh is like music. I have never really heard you laugh before."

In reply she dives under and kicks water into his face.

Lykeion dashes the water from his eyes, dives after her and grabs a foot. She twists free, an undulating naiad, bursting into the bright air, water droplets shimmering around her. She laughs at him again, then the moment is past. Whipping her wet hair back, she points at a stand of rushes swaying gently at the water's edge.

"There are your rushes, bard. Get to work on your pipes. I will wash our clothes and get some food ready. We have no time to waste."

The sun glints red on the river's surface as Lykeion hefts his simple pipes. Kiri looks up from the fish she is cooking with herbs over a small fire and nods.

"Will they work?"

He turns them over in his hands, tugs the tendril of grapevine holding the pipes together a little tighter.

"I think so. My mother taught me how to make these when I was small, but I have not made any in years." He blows into the hollow reed, and a small, sweet note mingles with the song of the river.

"Stop," Kiri commands. "You have done well. But no more yet." She stands, brushes off her hands, and plucks two broad leaves from the sycamore branch nodding over her head. Carefully, she pulls the fish from the fire and uses a stick to push an equal portion onto each leaf. The head and tail glint silver on a third leaf near the water. "Give the gods their portion, in the fire. Then eat. At dusk we will call Pan."

The reed music hops and skips over the chuckling waters of the river, a little hesitant at first, but growing in confidence and complexity. The moving water sparks ruby in the last flash of the sun and goes abruptly dark. Light lingers in the air, between the trees, playing with the wisps of smoke from the dying fire. The trees watch in silence.

The ritual area has been asperged with lustral water. The opening offerings and libations have been given. Lykeion picks up his pipes and nods at Kiri.

"Let us begin the summoning."

Kiri's feet begin to move in the soft sand of the river bank. Like the music they start slowly but catch the now-urgent rhythm. As they pack down the damp sand, her feet produce a faint drumming, counterpoint to the pipes. Her hair, loosed from its braid, whips around her as she bends from the waist, arches back, and spins.

The air thickens. The trees lean in. Lykeion begins to dance as well. The piping becomes ragged as his breath comes harder, but a wordless chant pours from the girl's throat, picking up the cadence, filling in the gaps. Bare feet beat a staccato tempo. The river tinkles like bells.

They whirl and stamp. The sky cools. The pipes squeak and whistle, but the dancing becomes more urgent. Their eyes are glazed, hair drenched with sweat. Kiri begins to moan, and now from her distended throat comes the ancient cry, over and over: "Io Pan! Io Pan! Io Pan! Io Pan!"

The boy's feet dig deeply into the sand as his dance halts abruptly. The simple pipes pierce the air along with Kiri's cries, urgent, compelling, pleading, commanding.

Kiri stops dancing as well. Her clenched fist pumps against the sky in time with her call. "Io Pan! Io Pan! Io Pan! Io Pan!"

The sycamores on the far side of the river rustle. One moment there are only the silent, watchful trees. In the next, a huge figure looms, horned head blotting out the early stars.

Yellow eyes stare down at the now-motionless pair at the river's edge. The oval irises narrow. A thick musk fills the humans' nostrils. The giant figure takes a step forward, emerging fully from the trees. His huge legs and haunches are those of a goat. His rampant member rises from between the hairy thighs.

But the voice is not the high-pitched bleat of a goat. It is deep and intensely male, with an undertone of wildness and violence that prick the boy and girl with primal terror. "Who summons me?"

Lykeion tries to loosen his tongue to reply, but his mouth has gone so dry that it seems stuck closed. He realizes with a start that the pipes are still between his lips. He pulls them away, but he still cannot free his tongue to speak. He steps forward, but the girl is swifter. Planting her feet apart and lifting her head so that her eyes meet the unblinking yellow ones so far above her, she lifts her hands, palms skyward, and speaks.

"O son of Hermes, beloved of nymphs and oreiads, who wanders through the thick woods and over steep crags, who dances among the crocus and fragrant hyacinth and sings by the dark spring, if ever we have pleased you as we have poured libations to you and your blessed Father, as we have sung our songs and tended our flock of goats, hear us now and help us in our hour of need. Areion has sent us to you in our desperation. O Pan, loud-roaring Pan, be propitious to us, and we will sing songs of you that will echo through the ages."

The yellow eyes flare and brighten. "You speak prettily, girl. And you name one whose coming my Father has foretold. Tell me, does this matter of desperation have aught to do with Areion's sister, She Who Must Not Be Named?"

The girl clasps her hands, kisses them and extends them back toward the God. "Oh, yes, my Lord, you know of this, then. Do you know of the terror spreading through the countryside? The deaths and desecration? And…." She stops, trembling. She regains control and continues in a shaky voice, "And the abomination of the children. She has taken the children and turned them into….something else. Not beasts, not humans, but things in a half-life, a life that goes against nature. We must save them."

A fat, yellow moon rises behind the great form of the god. He closes his eyes, then opens them, yellow like the moon.

"Children die. All mortals die when it is their time, child or ancient. I do not come between the All-Receiver and his due." He stands silent a while, Lykeion and Kiri also silent below him, frozen in fear. "But this is a violation of Law. Areion was right to send you." The boy and girl breathe again. Pan lowers his head toward them. "Does Poseidon Earth-Shaker know of this?"

"Yes," the girl replies. "He is doing what he can for the children. Some….some of them are still alive. But he is not stopping her. Maybe he cannot. I think that is why we need you."

The god shakes his shoulders with a noise like an impending rockslide. "Your need does not touch me. But Order must be restored." His nostrils flare as he thrusts his head toward them on the other side of the river. The musk scent becomes richer, ranker. Faint sounds can be heard in the forest behind the god. The noises bring a flush to the girl's cheeks; the boy is aghast to find himself suddenly fully erect.

A huge, cloven hoof steps into the river. "My retinue comes. Our revels may prove too vigorous for tender young morsels like you. Better fly." The other goat foot steps into the fast-flowing water. The god points to Kiri. "Bring the two who were born on the night of the Violation. The light and the dark. Bring them back to this place, on the dark of the moon."

Kiri gasps. "So long? I am afraid the children…." She stops abruptly as the bearded face splits into a grin, ivory and sharp in the moonlight.

"Will you argue? I will be there in a moment, my followers soon after. Do you think it wise to linger?"

His phallus twitches and strains forward, pulling the giant form another step into the river.

Before they can move or reply, the great head is thrown back, and the god roars. The trees bow, the river leaps, the sounds in the forest rise to an urgent cacophony. The two mortals scream in mindless terror and flee, leaving behind their few belongings with no thought but to escape.

Not until the sounds have been long left behind does sanity slowly seep back in. Kiri stops running, her breathing tearing. She grabs Lykeion's hand as he plunges toward a thicket of raspberries. He rounds on her, eyes wide, his other hand uplifted to strike, but he stops himself in mid-swing. They freeze, staring at each other. Lykeion takes a shaking breath.

"I am so sorry. I was not thinking. I—I could not

think. All I could do was try to get away. I have never been so crazed with fear before, never. Any rationality I possessed drowned in the roar of Pan. There was nothing but bright terror." He looks down at the ground, at his torn feet. "I was unmanned. I am ashamed."

Kiri does not release his hand. "We are mortals. We cannot stand up to that, not from a God." She shivers, not altogether with fear, thinking back on the sounds made by those who had been approaching the river. "I think he did us well in chasing us away. If we had not fled, it might have gone badly indeed." Her mouth twitches. "As it would had you run through those raspberry canes." She takes a step forward. "Oh! My feet!"

Lykeion sits heavily and pulls her down beside him. "Mine too. We left everything, but I do not think we can go back yet. I shall tear some strips off my tunic, and we can bind our feet. But then what?"

"Home," she replies. "We need supplies, and we need to get my goats."

"Your goats? Is that what he meant, the light and the dark?"

The moonlight makes black pits of her eyes, but Lykeion can see her chin tremble, just a little. Her voice, though, is firm.

"Yes. Two kids were born to my prize doe on the night I first saw the Goddess." Her eyes slide up to meet his. "But we cannot tell my family what has happened, what we have seen. Or what we are going to do. My father would not heed us; he would rush out to save the children. My mother....my mother cannot know what has befallen her boy. They would not wait. They could not. And Lykeion, we must do this as Areion and Pan have instructed. I do not know how any of the children can survive this ordeal. But if there is any chance, any chance at all that they will return to us, we have to trust that the Immortals are using us to make it happen."

Lykeion tries to imagine explaining to Stephanos what they have seen and done. He laughs, a small, rueful laugh. "I am not sure what would be worse, trying to tell them the truth, or trying to get them to cooperate with us without giving them any information at all. Your father might well throw me out, and not ever let you leave again. I do not think I would blame him."

Kiri is silent. Then she pushes herself painfully to her feet.

"Tear off some strips. There is enough light for me to gather some healing leaves in which to wrap our feet. We should rest until morning. It will take us about two days to reach my home. We will have to forage, but I know where to find good water. We're almost back in my family's grazing territory."

Lykeion teases a frayed bit of fabric with his nails,

grits his teeth and rips a strip off his already ragged tunic. "I hope those mainads do not wreck the place too badly. I left my lyre there, and I want it back!"

Chapter 8

BATHING

STEALING ONE'S OWN GOATS PROVES TO BE A harder task than Kiri has anticipated. Stephanos is not a man who can be easily misled, and the dogs are ferociously protective. Lykeion cups his hands around his mouth and delivers a convincing injured goat cry, luring Stephanos up the mountain, leaving the flock in the dogs' care. Kiri crouches in silence, barely breathing, in the woods overlooking the pasture. She waits until she can no longer hear Lykeion's plaintive bleats, then emerges cautiously from the trees near grazing goats and gives a low whistle. Three large, wolfish forms prick up their ears from their positions around the flock, then bound joyfully down to her, knocking her clear off her feet, whining and nosing and licking and rolling her around like a breathless puppy.

"Shh, shh," she tells them, shoving away eager noses. "Yes, I'm fine, I'm glad to see you too. Ow! Gently! You great idiots, give over." She grabs the lead dog, the big black-faced one, by the head and shakes him with rough love, and he croons at her.

The goats are interested now and begin moving toward them. Kiri stays on the ground, her arms full of dog, and lets them drift over to her quietly. She knows she must move with some alacrity but allows the goats and dogs to stay relaxed. The first one to reach her is the pure white golden-eyed buck. He butts his face into her, courteous with his short sharp horns, and bleats quietly. She scratches his ears.

"Hello, love. How is my Alexander?" He closes his golden eyes and chortles with ecstasy as she digs her nails under his chin. His sister, black as night with eyes of a startling pale blue, shoves him out of the way and demands her due. She blinks at Kiri and nibbles provocatively on her ragged tunic. "Melaina, you wretch, stop it, it is barely holding together as it is."

She glances anxiously up the mountain and gets to her feet. With a series of short, sharp gestures she sends the dogs, suddenly efficient and focused again, to herd the flock back up the field from the tree line. The two yearlings stay with her, grapevine cords around their necks. She signals to the dogs to stay with the flock. They watch, puzzled but obedient, as their mistress and the two goats slip away.

It is dusk before Lykeion steps into the grove of oaks where they planned to meet, miles from Kiri's home. He is so quiet that his footfalls do not wake them from their shared sleep, goats and girl tangled together in the tree roots. He keeps his breathing quiet and controlled as he looks at them, at Kiri's face wiped clean of the worry that has pinched it of late, at the slender limbs wound around the motionless forms of the goats. A starling cries out sharply from a branch overhead. The girl sighs and shifts. She does not wake, but the doe's blue eyes, blue even in the twilight, gleam at him.

"I wonder why the goats are needed?" he muses over the tiny fire later that evening. Kiri, chewing gamely on a mouthful of roasted root, does not answer right away. She swallows with some effort, and hands the rest of the charred chunk to Alexander, who takes it daintily from her fingers.

"I wish I knew," she says slowly. "None of this makes sense to me. But they were born on the night of the Goddess's ravishment. I suppose that bears some significance, but just what that is I cannot say." She tilts her head back and gazes up at the sky, veils of cloud trailing across the fields of stars. "Moondark is still a day away—but I do not feel as if we should wait. We should make our way to the river tomorrow."

One side of Lykeion's mouth twitches up. "If you feel we should, I shall not argue. You are bound into something I have never heard of before, not even in song or story. All I pray is that we both survive to hear the song I shall make of it if the gods allow." He pulls himself into a ball, facing the fitful flame. "If Pan does not want us there yet, I am sure He will let us know, one way or another."

Unseen, Kiri smiles—but it does not reach her eyes.

They rise early, their faces drawn and weary, the goats inscrutable. A shared bowl of hot tea and they set off, foraging for berries for their breakfast as they go. They walk all day, moving down from the highlands, down into the wooded glades that blanket the foothills from the river valley. They move steadily, not swiftly, allowing the goats to browse as they go. The trees become taller, with less shrubby undergrowth, and the walking is easy.

As the shadows begin to slant eastward and the bird song quiets in the afternoon heat, Kiri stops.

"I do not hear the river. Do you?"

Lykeion cocks his head, wearily waving away a determined mosquito. "No. But I have not been this way before. Should we?"

Kiri bites her lip, turns in a circle. "I would have thought so. Maybe not. If there are a few more hills between us and the river, that could be the reason. Let us continue southward. But keep your eyes and ears open. Something feels…." Her voice trails away.

"Feels what?" he prompts, eyeing the dozing trees warily.

She shakes her head. "I do not know. Maybe nothing."

He snorts. "Right now, I do not think there is any such thing as 'nothing' when it comes to you." He takes a firmer grip on his staff. "Come on. Let us see what it is that is making you so uneasy."

She scowls at him for a moment, then smiles suddenly and walks on. Melaina stops grooming Alexander's shoulder with her teeth, looks up at Lykeion with her strange eyes, and follows.

Later in the long afternoon Kiri stops in a little dell surrounded by irregular stones. Some loom over the clearing, tall and gaunt, like mad prophets. Others crouch as if turned to stone right before a leap. The earth between them is brown and parched, though the grass around is lush.

Kiri turns slowly. Lykeion and the goats stop at the verge of the woods, watching her uneasily.

"What is it?" says Lykeion. "I don't like this place."

Kiri shakes her head, her long braid writhing. She continues to pace around the sere patch of earth, studying the stones. She stops and gazes up at a tall fang of stone, its base littered with crumbled rock. Her eyes travel down the length of it and come to rest on a small, round boulder right at its foot. Lykeion watches, not realizing he is holding his breath. Kiri crouches down, never taking her eyes from the little boulder. The goats are motionless beside him, staring at her too, even the incessant movement of their jaws stilled.

The boulder stirs. A clawed foot stumps out from underneath it, and a wrinkled head unfurls. Bright, black eyes open and blink at the girl. They look at each other for what seems to Lykeion to be an eternity. Finally, the mountain tortoise turns its head from her and hoists itself up on all four of its feet. With a measured tread it lumbers away, out of the dell, heading west.

Kiri stands and looks back at Lykeion and the goats. "This is it. I need to follow him."

Lykeion takes a firmer hold of his staff and tugs on the grapevines around the goats' necks. "I am ready."

"No."

He gapes at her. She continues, "Tomorrow is moondark. Get to the river with the goats. I think....I think they are supposed to go there with you."

"Are you mad? You think after coming all this way with you, seeing all we have seen, I am just going to let you go off unprotected? Where you go, I go. I am not trying to stop you. If you say we are to follow a tortoise, I will follow it with you to the Isles of the Ionia, but I am coming with you. We," and he shakes the makeshift tether, causing Alexander to bleat in protest, "are all coming with you." He strides across the barren earth toward her.

"No," she says again, and something in her voice brings him up short. "I hope we will finish this together, for good or ill. But this is for me alone. You cannot come."

As Lykeion stares at her slight, erect form, the sun strikes a vein of mica in the standing stone behind her, and for a moment she is afire with sundazzle. He blinks and rubs startled water from his eyes. When he looks up again she is disappearing into the trees, following her guide. Her voice floats back to him.

"I will meet you back at the river." With a last flick of her braid, she is gone.

The goats butt him, complaining, pulling to get away from the stones. Still he stands, his hands clenching and unclenching. Finally, he drops his chin onto his breast. The goats tug him along, humming with relief, away from the stones.

"Stephanos would fell me with a single blow if he knew about this," he mutters to them as they pick their way southward.

The western sky has flamed through the trees, cooling as Kiri follows the tortoise around a bend on a steep, rocky hill. She is breathing hard, her throat parched. A little musical tinkle greets them. They hurry to the small pool that shimmers under a spring leaping from deep within the rock. Girl and tortoise drink deeply, side by side in the dusk, surrounded by the sound of living water. The overflow from the crystal pool spills down the hill, where it joins a stream and flows southward.

Toward the Ladon, thinks Kiri, cooling her wrists in the water and holding them to her temples. I believe I'm near the gorge of Neda. Impulsively, she untwists her dusty braid and dunks her whole head in the pool, finger-combing the floating strands of hair. She flings her head back, gasping, wet hair throwing droplets all over the tortoise, who immediately rises and moves determinedly to a dark crack in the face of the hill. Without a moment's hesitation, it stumps into the opening and disappears.

Kiri pushes aside a tangled curtain of wet hair, takes a single shaky breath and follows. The terror is no less than before, but this time it is clear that this is inevitable. The thought of turning back never enters her mind.

Nonetheless, a little bleat of fear erupts from her as the walls of the crack in the mountain begin to emit a pale, green glow. The tortoise glances back, then moves relentlessly forward, and she follows. The tight, sharp passage twists steeply down. The weight of the mountain hangs over her as she makes her way into its depths.

The passage ends abruptly, and the vast chamber leaps into cold green brilliance as Kiri steps in. Shadows race into the jagged ceiling far, far above. Stark in the icy light are two huge stone thrones and the figures sitting upon them.

Kiri's eyes cling to the immense female shape on the farther throne. She lifts her gaze from the beautifully formed feet, up past the dark robes draping the legs, the narrow waist, the deep breasts. Her eyes stop, appalled, at the head. The great, dark mare—not black, simply without light—stares back at her with crimson eyes. Eyes that hold nothing but seething rage. The hands are motionless on the armrests of the throne.

Demeter. The Great Mother.

In the seat on her left hand sits the Daughter, no longer a ghastly baby. But where the Mother is as still as the mountain itself, the Daughter flows and writhes like fog, like mist over a swamp. Her mare's head is also dark, but hard to look at. Later, much later, when trying to recall the scene, Kiri is unable to remember seeing eyes. But she knows she is watched, as a hawk watches a mouse. But no. Hawks hunt from hunger. The thing that is watching Kiri wants no less than the unraveling of Order itself, the perversion of Law, the onset of Chaos.

Kiri's gaze is deflected, bouncing off the gigantic figure like sleet hitting a frozen pond.

The juddering form of the Daughter rises.
Kiri falls, senseless, to the rock floor.

As Kiri follows the tortoise up the mountain path,
Lykeion makes his way steadily southward, the goats
trotting at his heels. The standing stones are not far
behind them when he hears the sound he has been
anticipating all through the long, hot afternoon—the
rush and jingle of the river. Melaina coos, fluttering
long lashes over her sky-colored eyes, and surges
ahead of Lykeion. Alexander leaps after her. Lykeion
lets go the tethers and follows them eagerly over a hill
and down a steep outcropping of rock. The three
young things line up on the river bank and have a
long, long drink.

When his thirst is slaked, Lykeion casts a practiced
eye at the sky, at the angle of the sun. He calls the
goats to him, and they begin to make their way
upriver, heading west. The goats protest and balk,
weary and wanting to forage, but Lykeion pushes them
along. They glare at him, snatching mouthfuls of
foliage as they march along the river bank.

Just as the sun slides behind the treetops, the
weary trio plods into a familiar clearing. Lykeion
bellows a shout of joy at the sight of his lyre leaning

against a rock by the cold ashes of their old fire and drops the goats' tether. Melaina and Alexander make satisfied grunts as they move to the riverbank shrubbery and start in on their dinner. Lykeion picks up his skin-wrapped instrument and strokes it, itching to unwrap it and make sure it is unharmed. But the sight of his abandoned makeshift reed pipes lying on the ground a few feet away brings him up short.

After a glance at the goats to make sure they are fully occupied with foraging he puts the lyre down reluctantly and walks slowly to the pipes. Involuntarily he glances across the darkening river to the spot where the goat-footed God had so recently towered. Only the trees move in the dark red light.

Lykeion puts the pipes to his lips and begins to play.

He sways on the sand of the riverbank. Time slips its tether. The goats dance with him. The trees rustle and hum to the tune of the pipes. The last light trembles on the edge of nightfall.

Lykeion realizes that other pipes have joined his, the rustic music weaving intricate patterns over the water. His eyes fly open wide, but he keeps the rhythm of the piping. The goats gambol about him. Figures emerge from the trees across the river, fantastical figures moving half-seen in the half-light. Men with horse tails, deer with the hands and hair of maidens, saplings with faces, huge hounds with red eyes, women with the ears and tails of foxes, all singing, dancing, some piping, some playing lyres or drums. Though his mouth goes dry with fear, still he plays, still he dances.

The throng on the far side of the river parts, and Pan comes through. His yellow goat eyes gleam. He halts at the river. His followers fall silent. Lykeion's pipes fall from nerveless fingers.

"The girl?" The deep voice holds no particular menace, but Lykeion feels his sinews loosen at the sound of it. He fights to stay upright.

"She follows a guide. I think it is taking her to the Demeter," he manages.

The yellow eyes sharpen and focus. "A guide came?"

Lykeion whispers, "A tortoise."

Pan flings back his head and the trees quiver with his laughter. "Father!" he bellows.

Lykeion finds himself weeping into the deep riverbed sand, clutching handfuls of it. He forces his eyes open, and across the darkening water he can see and hear the god's followers, wailing, shrieking, laughing, fighting, and, he realizes before squeezing his eyes shut, copulating.

When he opens his eyes, he finds himself nose to nose with a mountain tortoise. The hooded eyes blink at him. From far above them a voice says, "Prepare the sacrifice."

There is a clatter on the stones nearby. A curved

knife catches a gleam from the fading light.

By the time Lykeion gets to his knees in the damp sand the tortoise is disappearing through the trees. A huge goatish form moves with it.

The goats move close to him. Melaina rubs her head against his leg. He scratches behind her ear and looks at the blade.

The cacophony across the water has not abated by the time Lykeion finishes bathing the goats. He stands naked in the sand, rubbing Alexander dry with his ragged tunic, trying to ignore the sounds and the ribald invitations from the heaving shadows on the far side of the river. He kneels and rubs his hands all over the little buck's body, making sure that it is perfectly clean and smooth. Then he leads him to the undergrowth where Melaina is grazing placidly.

Lykeion starts to don the damp sandy tunic, throws it aside and sits on a rock with his feet in the water. The stars wheel overhead.

The shrieks and wet slapping sounds suddenly cease. Lykeion jerks his head up.

A satyr steps onto the river bank carrying a limp, slender form in its arms. He dumps it, not ungently, onto the sand next to the boy, grins wickedly and disappears into the trees.

Lykeion feels his chest unclench for the first time since Kiri walked away from him so many hours before. He flings himself onto the sand beside her, murmuring her name, gently pushing the hair from her face. When she moves, opens her eyes and looks back at him, he almost weeps aloud. He lifts her head with his arm, cradles her against his chest.

Kiri reaches up with one hand and touches his face. She does not speak. She closes her eyes for just a moment. Then she pushes herself away and gets to her knees, facing the woods.

The revelers pour across the starlit river, fording it as easily as if it were a mountain rill. They strew the sand with ferns and fronds, from the tree line down to the bank of the darkly swirling river. When they have finished creating a fragrant pathway, they withdraw and stand to either side of it, silent and expectant.

The trees sway against the stars, and part. The goat-footed god paces slowly from under the canopy. He escorts a goddess, whose hand rests lightly on his arm. A dark robe envelops her form. From the high cowl emerge the long neck and head of a great mare. The ears swivel forward, then back. Crimson eyes regard the double line of beings standing at attention and flare lividly.

Pan halts. His retinue, as one, makes a deep obeisance. He gently lifts the goddess' hand from his arm and moves to face her. He lowers his horned head gracefully, touches his right hand to his forehead, and extends it to her. Then he looks her full in the face, into those terrible eyes, and grins, a grin of shimmering delight, of wicked pleasure, of unbridled admiration, of boundless respect. One of her flattened ears pricks forward. Then the other. He reaches out with both hands, takes hers, and begins to draw her toward the water, stepping backward between the motionless rows of fantastic creatures.

And she follows him.

As they move toward the river, another figure steps out from the trees. Like Demeter she is tall, dark-robed, horse-headed. But while the mother goddess is solid, shapely—mesmerizing even—in her dreadfulness, it is hard to look at the daughter. Her outline twists, and mists coil around her, or perhaps flow off her. Her red eyes roll in her head, her great rectangular teeth gnash. Her arms extend toward her Mother, fingers convulsing.

Kiri's heart contracts. She starts to rise, to go to the shuddering form making its way between the recoiling retinue, but Lykeion pulls her hand, holding it to his breast.

"It's out of our hands. Be still. Watch."

To his surprise, she complies.

Demeter has reached the river. Dark water swirls around Pan's hairy knees as he steps backward, guiding her in. She keeps her hands in his, but halts before her feet touch the water. She turns back toward her daughter. The throbbing red eyes dim, and for a long moment they are dark and sad.

Tears spring from Kiri's eyes and pour down her face.

The daughter staggers. The entire clearing seems to blur. Her hands, like claws, clench and stretch desperately. She totters forward a few more steps, making sounds that are a ghastly echo of a filly's anxious nicker. Her ears flick rapidly back and forth.

"Come," says the deep voice of Pan. Demeter turns her horse head back toward him. For a long moment, she stands motionless on the bank. Then she steps into the water. Her eyes flare so brilliantly that Lykeion and Kiri clap their hands over their own eyes. When they look again, the goddess is completely submerged in the river, Pan standing protectively over her.

The daughter shrieks.

She lifts her hands and rakes them down her face. Furrows open and run red under the staring eyes, down the long, bony face to the flared nostrils. She rips at her garments, tearing and rending, revealing glimpses of a perfect female form wracked and twisted appallingly as she writhes. Every being on the shore draws back in horror, leaving the tortured figure to arch and gibber alone on the sand, blood streaming and puddling around her.

Mists rise from the red pools, mercifully veiling the

twitching and flopping. Then, with one long shuddering wail, she falls silent. The form begins to dissolve, to melt, to slowly slide into a wet gelatinous mound.

Kiri bites back a scream, remembering the birth.

As the melting horse head slides into the heaving pile of ooze, the eyes lock onto Kiri's. Without warning, the awful equine head is gone, and in its place is the face of a girl, a flower-faced girl of such exquisite, innocent beauty that every being on the shore of the river stops breathing.

The scent of flowers fills the air.

And then she is gone. The dark, gleaming mass heaves one last time and dissolves into the earth.

Kiri wails, bereavement shredding her throat.

An answering cry reverberates from the river.

Demeter arises.

The dark mare's head is gone. The gorgeous sweep of neck ends in the head of a woman, but never a mortal. As the last of the glistening heap disappears, she throws back her head with a cry of grief so profound that every being on the river bank falls prostrate, sobbing. Only Pan remains erect, motionless, holding the space for her. Her head is thrown back, as if the wealth of hair is too much for the long neck to support.

Overhead, the stars wink out, one by one.

She takes a step toward the shore. Her dark robes

have vanished. She is stupendously nude, water streaming from her shoulders and breasts. She takes another step, and a group of nymphs come forward with a pure white linen garment in which to receive her.

As her form is adorned, the goddess turns a face of sublime sweetness to Kiri and Lykeion. Eyes of a deep, rich, warm green rest on their grimy faces. They are bathed in love, a laughing, wondering, delighted, all-encompassing love. It fills them to overflowing.

"Make the sacrifice," says Pan.

Kiri tears her eyes away from the grass-green eyes of the goddess and stares at Lykeion.

"What sacrifice?" she whispers.

He moves his head slightly, indicating something behind her. She turns. Facing her, standing squarely in the sand, are Melaina and Alexander. Blue eyes and gold stare unblinkingly into hers. The goats are utterly still, not even chewing their cud.

Kiri's eyes fly back to Lykeion. He nods, looking steadily at her, and picks up the scythe. She takes two running steps toward him, reaching for the scythe. He puts out a quelling hand, his eyes never leaving her face. Her hands fly to her mouth. She shakes her head, tears welling.

Holding her gaze, Lykeion says in a low voice, "It is for the children."

For a long moment she returns his look, then nods.

"It is also for the goddess," she whispers. She goes to her goats, takes Alexander's head into her hands, and begins to hum to him. Her fingers find his favorite spot, right behind his white ears, and scratch just how he likes it. His golden eyes close in bliss.

The knife flashes in the growing light.

Melaina does not move when they turn to her.

"Bring them," says Pan.

Kiri picks up Alexander's limp body. Lykeion sets the scythe carefully down and lifts the gleaming black form that was Melaina.

Under the eyes of the Goddess, of Pan, of the assorted beings of the retinue, they carry the bodies of the little goats into the river that flows almost up to Pan's goatish flank.

"Let them go," says the God, and they release the sacrifices into the current. The river washes the blood from their hands and faces as they wade back to the shore.

Kiri falls to her knees in the damp sand. Her hands hang limply at her sides. She stares blankly in front of her.

The scent of grass and summer envelops her. A touch on her chin lifts her face, and she finds herself gazing into the shimmering green and gold eyes of the goddess. The few remaining stars gather over Demeter's bright head.

"You have done well, brave little doula. Order

returns. The surviving children shall be restored." A finger moves up to Kiri's cheek, caresses it. Tears dazzle Kiri's eyes.

When she can see again, Lykeion is beside her, staring across the river. In the growing light of daybreak, a moving object can be seen coming through the trees. Satyrs are pulling something, something that gleams bright gold, gems flashing a rainbow of colors. A chariot on two wheels that seem to be made of spider silk and sunlight is brought to the water's edge and left, gleaming.

Pan moves from the river to the bank. He lowers his great, horned head, inspects the chariot, nods to himself. As he draws in a huge breath, expanding his massive chest, Kiri and Lykeion cover their ears just in time before his bellowing summons shakes the river itself.

And from the roiling surface rise two pairs of horns, one as white as summer clouds, one as black as the space between the stars. Up, up from the water the two creatures rise, horned, bearded, turning familiar blue and golden eyes upon the humans crouching on the shore. But only the eyes are familiar. The goat heads are poised on long slender necks. Water pours from the emerging shoulders, black and white. Wings unfurl, scattering drops of water over everyone on the shores. Serpentine tails whip out of the river, coiling and striking.

Kiri cries out, "Alexander! Melaina!" and stretches a hand toward the creatures. But nothing in them indicates the slightest sign of recognition. Kiri drops her hand, confused, shaken, dazzled.

Pan rumbles low in his throat. The dragons move out of the river and go to him. They do not touch him. Their cold, beautiful eyes move from him to the chariot. The black dragon spreads her wings, which sparkle, iridescent, in the dawn, then folds them against her back. She and the white dragon move to the front of the chariot.

Pan harnesses them to it with straps of gold. They stand in the pale pink light—goat horns and heads, goat beards, cloven goat hooves, but the wings and tails of dragons.

Demeter steps to the shore, gleaming and glorious. Pan comes to her, takes her hand and escorts her across the moving waters. She is tall, so tall, her golden head seeming to tower above the trees, but she steps lightly onto the surface of the water and treads across the river as if it were a meadow path. Pan hands her into the chariot and gives her the reins.

She looks back for just a moment, back across the river, and her gaze meets Kiri's tear-bedazzled eyes. She smiles, and the sun comes up. Brilliance fills the air. In the light, the dragons spread their wings and leap upward. All the members of the retinue bow deeply.

Pan lets loose one of his great shouts.

Kiri and Lykeion are knocked to the ground by the force of the shout. They lie next to the river in the ordinary light of morning.

Chapter 9

DENOUEMENT

LYKEION AND KIRI SIT IN THE SUN ON A BOULDER overlooking the upland pasture, dotted with grazing goats. The three big dogs lie nearby in the deep shade of an olive grove, their sides rising and falling rapidly, eyes half-closed, mouths wide and grinning. Across the mountain, trees begin to glow yellow and red, but the afternoon is hot and still. Even the insects seem drowsy in the heat. The only movement comes from a pair of dragonflies darting above the pasture, wings shimmering.

Kiri stretches and sighs. Lykeion glances at her, half smiling.

"Even without Melaina and Alexander, it is a good little herd," he says gently. "The cheese you have been making is exceptional."

Kiri does not reply. She settles her chin in her hand and traces a line of moss growing in a crack in the boulder, cool and lime green, with surprising tiny pink flowers. The damp moss leaves a green stain on her fingertip, and she tries without success to scrub it off on the rough stone.

"Mother and I are attending the wife of a man on the far side of Wolf Fang Mountain. She will come to her childbed around the grape harvest. They breed good black goats and have promised to give us one. I may never find a doe as good as Amalthea again, but I will pick a nice one." She flicks a pebble moodily at the dogs, who grin even more widely at her. "Oh, what does it matter? They are just goats. Not like...." she breaks off and rubs her eyes angrily. Then she glances up at Lykeion, who still regards her softly, and smiles ruefully. "Forgive me, my friend. I don't know what comes over me sometimes."

Before he can reply, a cascade of raucous shrieks rolls across the drowsy pasture. The goats startle and draw together in a nervous circle, but the dogs only lift their ears and continue to pant. A tiny figure of a girl staggers down the little mountain path, falls to her hands and knees, lets loose a peal of high-pitched laughter and begins to crawl rapidly through the dry grass. Behind her appears a small boy, grabbing her by a plump rosy leg and pretending to bite it. They roll in the dust like puppies, screaming and gasping.

The darkness lifts from Kiri's face in an instant. She leaps to her feet. "Patrokles! What are you doing to poor Kiri-ke? You two are going to scatter the goats all over the mountain, hush now."

Lykeion clasps his hands around a knee and watches, smiling, as Kiri runs up the hill to the two children, her hair flying out behind her, and gathers them both into her arms, kissing and nuzzling them until they shriek even more loudly.

"You are worse than they are," he calls to her. "Noisy and naughty!" His smile fades. "Not even a moon ago we found them, still on that beach," he murmurs to himself. "Frightened, hungry and lost. Some of them dead." He gets to his feet and whistles up the dogs. "But at least they had their own heads again." As Kiri and the babies fall into a laughing heap in the shade, he and the dogs slowly gather the alarmed goats and begin to move them up the hill toward Stephanos's home.

Stephanos looks up from the stone wall on which he is working as Kiri crests the hill with an armful of children, trailed by Lykeion and goats and dogs. He straightens, knuckles his back, grimaces, then grins suddenly.

"Kephalos!" he calls. "The young scamps snuck away from the women yet again. We may have to devise hobbles for them."

Kephalos comes from around the corner, where he

has been working out the logistics of creating an interior door. "At least little Kiri-ke is being carried by someone big enough to lift her. Not that she minds Patrokles dragging her about in the dirt. Eleni! Look at our daughter! She's got the dust of half the mountain in her hair!"

Eleni runs out of the hut, exclaims in consternation, and hurries to relieve Kiri of half her burden. But as soon as the tiny girl is in her mother's arms, Patrokles squirms to get down and follows Eleni into the shelter, holding Kiri-ke's plump little leg. Aglaia steps aside to let them enter, putting out a hand to stroke Patrokles' dark curly head. She smiles a little uncertainly at her daughter as Kiri comes slowly toward the home.

"Since you brought them home, the only person these two have any use for other than each other is you. It is a good thing that Kephalos and Eleni are willing to leave the mountain peak and live with us. I think Patrokles would make his way right up to that cave by himself if we tried to keep him from Kiri-ke."

Kiri smiles back at her mother, knowing that her moodiness of late has caused Aglaia concern. The strangeness that has been upon her since she and Lykeion returned has made it difficult for her to fit back into her normal family life.

"Sharing a hearth with Eleni and Kephalos is a good thing for both our families. I love having Kiri-ke so close. She is precious to me."

A cloud passes briefly over her face, but she shakes it off with an effort that does not escape her mother.

"Well," says Aglaia briskly, "that is to be expected, but I think Karissa is a little jealous of your bond with that baby. Do not forget to give some attention to your sister."

"I am not," says Karissa breathlessly, coming around the corner of the house carrying two tightly woven baskets of water from the spring. "This is to bathe Kiri-ke as well as start dinner." She continues pointedly, "Kiri midwived Kiri-ke. She rescued her and all the other children. Kephalos and Eleni named her after Kiri. Of course they have a bond. I am not a baby. I understand things." She lifts a firm little chin and marches into the hut.

Kiri's eyes meet her mother's and they both smile.

"These girls of mine!" Aglaia exclaims. "Hearts of lions!"

"Indeed," says Eleni, emerging with a slightly less dusty Kiri-ke in her arms, Patrokles still attached like a limpet to her side. Her pale face is unsmiling as she strokes her baby's cheek. "We have good men. Strong men. But none of the men of this countryside were able to protect our children—or rescue them. Kiri says little about it, but she and that boy did what no one else was able to do. I am proud that my little girl is named for her. I hope she grows up with the lion heart your children have, Aglaia."

Kephalos comes out of the hut as his wife speaks. When she finishes, he gently takes the baby from her and tucks her, bright-faced and tousled, into the crook of his arm. He looks soberly at Kiri.

"I will never forget the sight of the two of you coming over the hill with sun behind you, and all those children. Our children."

"Not all, though," Kiri says quietly.

Her mother gathers Kiri's loose hair, twists it in her hands and pulls, not gently.

"Are you a goddess, that you can rule over life and death? You killed no one. You brought many who were thought to be lost back to their parents' arms. It is foolish to despair over what you cannot control. You are not foolish, my girl."

She releases Kiri's hair. Kiri pulls it sharply over her shoulder and turns her back. Karissa peeks, wide-eyed, out of the hut. Aglaia stands silently. Kiri glances back at her, smiles ruefully.

"No. You would not let me be."

"Kiri!" pipes Kiri-ke and stretches out her arms to Kiri, wiggling.

Kiri's smile brightens. Kephalos sighs and hands his daughter to her namesake.

"Well, at least she still lets us feed her and put her to bed."

Kiri swings the baby onto her shoulders, and the

two head toward the goat pen. Patrokles streaks out of the hut, skims around his mother's grasp and joins them, just as Lykeion and the dogs come around the corner.

"I've been helping my father and Kephalos make the house bigger!" says Patrokles, inflating his little chest. "Where are you going to sleep when it's finished, Lykeion? Will you be within our walls?"

Lykeion lifts his eyes to Kiri's. She meets his gaze for a moment, then drops hers in confusion. Without taking his eyes from her face, Lykeion says slowly, "I need to speak to you all."

One huge star preens in the purple sky as the two families stand on a rise, watching Lykeion pick his way down the mountain path. Only Karissa has refused to come see him off. She turned her back to him when he came to find her, hitting his outstretched hand with a hard little fist, then ran into the hut, sobbing furiously.

Stephanos picks up Patrokles, who lays his head on his father's shoulder and whimpers. They turn back home, and slowly the others follow. Only Kiri remains, watching the lone figure grow smaller against the darkening trees. He pauses for a moment at the verge of the whispering woods. Without looking back, he disappears between the trees.

Kiri's hand tightens on the stone he gave her just a short time before. It is a rough oval, small enough to fit in her palm, with a swirl down the center dividing it in two. Half the stone is a matte black so dense it seems to utterly absorb all light that touches it. The other half is a white so pure it reminds her of the big star setting in the west. He had pressed it into her hand, hard enough to hurt, and murmured, "It is like your goats, so different, yet fitting perfectly together. And maybe like—" he paused and looked down. After a moment he went on, "I have to go. Like your little goats, I have to become more. I must spread the story of the Goddesses in the cave. And to create the song, I must go and do nothing but listen in silence until the song is given to me. But when I have it, when I am ready to sing it fully, I will come back. Will you be here?"

For the first time, she had found it hard to hold his gaze. "I do not know. I think so." Her breath caught. "I think so."

"I hope so." There had been a depth of longing in his voice that surprised them both. His hand had lifted, but did not quite touch her face.

Kiri looks at the stone. The white side catches the faint early starlight and gleams, while the black side seems to dissolve into her hand. Closing her fingers over it, she turns from the woods down the mountain to the crest above, outlined against the purple eastern sky.

The rhythmic thud of hoofbeats thrums through the cicada song. A dark shape is briefly silhouetted against the disc of the rising moon. Green glimmers flow along its mane and tail.

Kiri stops, not breathing, as the dark horse strides deliberately toward her. He halts before her, facing her with a white-rimmed emerald eye. But the now-familiar voice still vibrates with an undercurrent of laughter.

"So, little doula. You have done rather well, you and the boy. Children freed from a half-life of horror, the Mother from her fury, the Despoina from her agony. Few mortals can look upon the sights you have seen and live. Do you feel triumphant?"

"No," she whispers to him, so low that his ears swivel forward to catch the sound. "I am glad Patrokles and Kiri-ke are restored to themselves, and the others who survived, too. I can hardly bear to think about the goddess, or Pan, or the cave. I do not understand any of it, and I am so glad the great mother goddess, the dapple-gray mare, is whole and herself again. But I do not seem to fit into my life anymore. I do not know what to do. And Lykeion...."

Her head droops. Her shoulders start to shake.

They are both silent for a time on the hillside as it silvers under the rising moon. After a time, Kiri dries her face on her arm and looks up at the stallion. He swings his narrow head from her and stares back at the hilltop. His nostrils flare, and he nickers sharply.

A slender shape crests the hill and comes slowly toward them on four delicate legs. The filly stops a few paces behind Areion, silver with dapples like dark wisps of cloud. She shakes her forelock from wide, suspicious eyes and snorts loudly. A foreleg slim as a willow wand reaches out and paws the ground with a small silver hoof. Her nostrils widen. She extends her head toward Kiri and takes a noisy sniff. Kiri does not move. She does not blink or even breathe. Entranced, she watches the wide, wild eyes take her in and slowly lose some of the wariness. The filly takes a slow step forward, presses herself against Areion's side. He nuzzles her ear, then playfully seizes her crest in his teeth and shakes gently. She squeals, pulls free, and moves another step closer to Kiri.

Letting her breath out slowly, Kiri reaches a hand toward the filly and holds it still. The filly's ears flick backward and her body tenses. One ear comes forward, then the other. Lips as soft as pussy willows touch Kiri's outstretched palm. Quivering, Kiri forces herself to remain motionless as the questing lips move up her arm, pause to chew briefly on her hair, then release sweet breath into her neck. Slowly, slowly she lifts her hand and strokes the shining curve of neck, feeling the play of muscle under the satin skin. She turns her head and inhales right behind the velvety ear, breathing in the intoxicating fragrance. The huge, dark eye looks deeply into her. The filly sighs and blows down Kiri's bodice, making Kiri laugh, which startles them both. It breaks their rapt absorption with each other, and they look up to see Areion moving away, heading downhill toward the forest.

The filly nickers after him but does not move from Kiri's side.

"Areion!" calls Kiri. "Will she stay with me?"

He does not stop or turn his head. His voice floats back. "If you treat her well, I suppose so. My sire sends her, with his thanks. He is her sire, too, so you may discover she has talents other horses do not possess. Farewell, little doula."

"Will I ever see you again?" she cries out, suddenly heartbroken all over again.

"No," comes the response. The blackness of the trees has entirely enveloped him. Only the strange green of his mane and tail are still visible.

"Does she have a name?"

"Yes," floats back on the moonlit air, and he is gone.

The filly neighs in sudden panic, rears up and leaps into a gallop down the hill after him. But after a few strides she catches herself and slides to a halt. Head high, she prances in place, staring into the trees. Then she whirls and races back up the slope to Kiri, skidding to a halt before her, shaking her long mane and snorting a little. Kiri rubs her between her wide, dark eyes, slides her other hand along the proud curved neck and scratches her withers. The filly sighs happily, waggles her upper lip and stretches around to rub it on Kiri's arm.

They stand together for a while, listening to the night.

The Source of the Story

The ancient stories tell of the goddess Demeter, who wanders, forlorn, through the region of Arkadia, mourning the loss of her daughter. The maiden Kore has been abducted by the God of the Underworld who has taken her to be his Queen of the Dead, where her loving mother cannot follow. Demeter's grief cannot be assuaged.

Even in mourning her boundless beauty remains. As she drifts about the countryside, Poseidon, god of the sea, espies her. Thunderstruck with desire, he pursues her relentlessly, refusing to accept her adamant refusal. Desperate, she transforms herself into a mare and mingles with the wild herds of the Arkadian plains, hoping to lose herself in the multitudes. But Poseidon cannot be so easily eluded. He turns himself into a great stallion and stalks her until he captures and ravishes her.

The beautiful face of the goddess becomes fury incarnate. As embodied fury, she gives birth to two offspring from the violent union. One is a horse named

Areion, with a green mane and tail and the power of human speech. The other is a dreadful daughter, whose name can never be uttered. She is referred to in the ancient sources only as 'Despoina,' which means 'mistress.'

A reign of terror descends upon the region of Arkadia—screams in the night, children disappearing from their beds. The folk of Arkadia, in desperation, call upon the wild god Pan to intercede on their behalf. Pan persuades the Raging Goddess to bathe in the River Ladon. Her terrible anger and pain are washed away, and peace returns to the countryside.

For ages there was a cave cult in Arkadia where two Goddesses were worshipped. Their cult statues depicted them as female forms with the heads of mares.

Areion shows up briefly in other myths, principally connected with Herakles. The Despoina is mentioned only in conjunction with her Mother.

References and Further Reading

Guide to Greece Volume 2: Southern Greece by Pausanias. Book VIII Chapter 37, 'Arkadia,' and Chapter 42, 'Mount Elaius.'

Eleusis: Archetypal Image of Mother and Daughter by Carl Kerenyi. Page 70 'For there, in Arcadia, Artemis was the sister and Poseidon the father of Persephone.'

Women of Classical Mythology by Robert E. Bell. Page 162 'Despoena.'

Library by Apollodorus. Book 3, Chapter 6, Section 8. Brief mention of Areion's birth at the end of the section.

The Iliad by Homer. Book 23 Line 392. Areion reference.

About the Author

Suz Thackston is a weird old mystic who mutters to trees and puts bowls of honey out for the fae. She lives on little Moonshadow Farm with her nice husband, a sweet dog, a couple of pampered lazy mares and some really bossy cats. She absentmindedly steps through portals, wanders into mists and gets lost in looking glasses. Don't send help.